*Ecstasy Romance* ®

## "DO YOU JUDGE YOUR PATIENTS, TOO?" JONATHAN CHALLENGED.

"If you don't like their business practices do you kick them out of your office? Or do you reserve that privilege for the bedroom?" he snapped.

"I don't sleep with my patients!" Rose Ellen yelled back. "And I don't judge them. But it's different with you because I care about you . . . about us. And I think I'm in love with you . . ."

"You're in love with me. That's very flattering. But I'm not sure you know what that means. If you love somebody, you support him. You give him the benefit of the doubt. You believe in him. You've got a lot to learn about love . . . about the world," he said sadly.

"What do you want me to do? Beg your forgiveness. I won't because maybe you're not sure about us either," she countered, defiance in her tone.

"Maybe," he agreed cuttingly. "For a while I thought I was. But you're right. I'm not sure anymore despite your pretty avowal of love—everlasting or not. I'm going home now, Rose Ellen," he said, slamming the door behind him.

# A CANDLELIGHT ECSTASY ROMANCE ®

# LOVE'S MADNESS

*Sheila Paulos*

A CANDLELIGHT ECSTASY ROMANCE ®

Published by
Dell Publishing Co., Inc.
1 Dag Hammarskjold Plaza
New York, New York 10017

*Verse on page 27 courtesy of
my father-in-law, Peter Paulos.*

Dell ® TM 681510, Dell Publishing Co., Inc.
Candlelight Ecstasy Romance®, 1,203,540, is a registered
trademark of Dell Publishing Co., Inc.,
New York, New York.

ISBN: 0–440–14727–1

Printed in the United States of America
First printing—November 1983

To Our Readers:

We have been delighted with your enthusiastic response to Candlelight Ecstasy Romances®, and we thank you for the interest you have shown in this exciting series.

In the upcoming months we will continue to present the distinctive sensuous love stories you have come to expect only from Ecstasy. We look forward to bringing you many more books from your favorite authors and also the very finest work from new authors of contemporary romantic fiction.

As always, we are striving to present the unique, absorbing love stories that you enjoy most—books that are more than ordinary romance.

Your suggestions and comments are always welcome. Please write to us at the address below.

Sincerely,

The Editors
Candlelight Romances
1 Dag Hammarskjold Plaza
New York, New York 10017

# CHAPTER ONE

RoseEllen Robbins, psychologist, sighed resignedly as she surveyed the crowded room. Gala black-tie affairs always made her uncomfortable. She preferred to spend her evenings curled up with a book or watching a TV movie or talking with friends. But attendance at these functions was important for her career. They were a good source of contacts, which meant more referrals, and this one was being hosted by the very influential Dr. Fred Riley to kick off the opening of his new clinic.

The dazzling room, the Louis Philippe Terrace, had been rented in one of Philadelphia's posh catering establishments. It was aglitter with mirrored walls, crystal chandeliers shimmering in their own light, and the sound of champagne glasses clinking. Living up to their reputation as party givers par excellence, the Rileys had spared no expense in throwing this bash. White-shirted waiters bearing trays of smoked oysters and caviar canapés were ubiquitous. A five-piece band played music that made even the lead-footed among the guests feel like John Travolta, while the soft lighting made worry lines and wrinkles disappear. A glimpse at the clothing worn by some of the guests would have made the buyer at Nan Duskin, Philadelphia's most exclusive department store, crow with joy.

RoseEllen, her long chestnut hair plaited in a French braid, wore an understated black halter dress of clingy crepe that emphasized both the slimness of her hips and the fullness of her breasts. She was oblivious to the numerous appreciative male glances sent her way. She stood on the outskirts of a group of older colleagues, men with horn-rimmed glasses and tufts of gray hair growing out of their ears, who would surely have been more at home in well-worn tweed than in mothball-preserved tuxedos. They were discussing a paper recently published in the *Journal of Family Therapy* with less than their usual animation, for their glances kept returning to the alluring therapist in their midst whom they had never before seen in anything other than tailored blouses, pleated skirts, and a no-nonsense manner. That some of their thoughts were centered more on erotica than esoterica finally registered on RoseEllen's consciousness when she realized that for the last ten minutes one eminent psychologist had been addressing a monologue on new techniques of self-help to her décolletage.

Reaching out to a passing waiter with his tray of champagne, RoseEllen exchanged her empty glass for a full one. Her glance swept the room. With gilded mirrors on all four walls it was hard to know where the room began and where it ended, or who the real people were and which were images. To her unpracticed eye everyone looked glamorous and at ease. Compared to the other women, with their Spanish lace and antique satin gowns, she felt underdressed. But RoseEllen didn't possess a large wardrobe and what she had was simple. Frills and flounces weren't her style. Or maybe they were and she just didn't know it.

The tiny hairs at the back of her neck prickled. It was the kind of sensation she sometimes got when someone she knew was about to accost her on the street or when her phone was about to ring. RoseEllen usually claimed laughingly that she was living proof that extrasensory perception did exist. Expecting to greet an old friend, she looked around her. People were laughing, flirting, making deals, but no one seemed to be bearing down on her. She shrugged. The sensation must just have been one of those things. Maybe it was the air conditioning, which was set to freeze ice cubes, she thought.

Her eye was caught by the mirrored reflection of a dowager decked in diamonds. She thought lightly that if that lady decided to divest herself of her jewels the whole price structure of the diamond market would have to be reset. Next to the woman was a group of young people looking as awed by the display of wealth as RoseEllen was. She hoped that she, however, wore a suitably blasé expression. Next to a large fern she spotted a man, his head bent as he lit a cigarette. In the most uncanny way her eyes became riveted on the figure. If there were such a thing as instant physical attraction this was it, and it hit her like a lightning bolt. With his longish blue-black hair that was prematurely gray at the temples, his square jaw that went oddly well with the strongly molded bones of his face, a mouth that was hard as if used to issuing commands, and his tall, muscular physique, apparent even through the shirt and jacket he wore, he was simply the most compelling man she had ever seen. He straightened up and and as he did so it seemed to her that he looked straight at her. Quickly she averted her glance. She had that strange feeling at the back of her neck again. She took a sip of her champagne. When she looked up again a young blond woman was giggling up at him. RoseEllen took the opportunity to study the gentleman at her leisure. He walked over to the bar behind him to fetch a drink for his companion, his movements marked with the utmost confidence and grace. He wore an indolent expression on his face and it occurred to RoseEllen that he was the type of man who was too well aware of the effect he created upon women. The blonde was following him to the bar, probably, RoseEllen thought, to avoid the risk of his not returning. With a clarity that belied the fact that she was a contact lens wearer, RoseEllen observed the tiny lines around the corners of his eyes. He was a man in his early thirties, she thought, the type of man to whom the years would be especially kind. All that was fine, she mused, as his image crowded everything else out of the room, but there were lots of attractive men in the world. No, there was something else about this man; it was a feeling that he possessed a power, a command, a total assurance. Without warning he looked up again and his eyes, dark and unflinching in the mirror, caught her. She had the feeling that he was undressing her with his eyes, that he saw more than was his right. Her cheeks burned and her hand trembled, causing a dash of champagne to spill on her open-toed silver sandal. His stare remained fixed on her, though she could see his blond companion was talking rapidly to get his attention. She wanted to look away but couldn't. She was powerless under his intense gaze. When after a long second he took his eyes from hers in the mirror, RoseEllen thought fleetingly of someone ripping apart a giant magnet and a metal jack, the kind that children play with. She moved jerkily away from the spot where she had stood as if pinioned. Circulate, she had to circulate. She headed for the buffet table that groaned with its platters of poached salmon, giant shrimp, goose pâté with truffles flown in from the south of France, and so many other delectable foods. The dessert table next to it looked as if it were part of a layout for *Better Homes and Gardens*.

"Mind if I join you?"

Even before RoseEllen whirled around she knew who it was. He was even more devastating at close range. His voice was well modulated, with a velvety quality to it.

"Sure. I, uh, was just going to nibble on some shrimp," she stammered.

"Excellent idea." He took the plate from her, picked one up for himself, and loaded them with the shellfish. "There's a table over there." He led the way to a small table with two chairs.

RoseEllen found herself following. He held out a chair for her.

"What's your name?"

"RoseEllen Robbins."

"I'm Jonathan Wood. Hello."

"Hello." For the first time in years RoseEllen was tongue-tied. She had no idea what to say next.

"You're a beautiful woman. Do you know that?"

RoseEllen flushed. "Are you a colleague of Dr. Riley?" she asked, in a voice that sounded, to her own ears, quavery and unsure.

"Hell no," he laughed. It was a rich, mellow sound. "That's the last thing I'd be, though I am here on business."

"Oh," RoseEllen responded in a small voice. "What sort of business are you in?"

"Junk. I'm a junkman." He grinned.

His words brought about a sinking sensation. RoseEllen had made a mistake. Obviously she and this man had nothing in common. Like any impressionable adolescent she had been taken in by his looks. She chewed thoughtfully on a shrimp that was tasteless and rubbery in her mouth.

His smile broadened as he watched her with interest.

11

RoseEllen prayed that her face, which was usually quite readable, had not displayed the gamut of her emotions.

"Who did you come with?" he probed.

"Myself."

"You're not the date of an illustrious so-and-so, then? Good," he pronounced with satisfaction.

"I *am* an illustrious so-and-so," she responded spitefully.

"You certainly are," he agreed heartily. "Lovely, just lovely."

RoseEllen fumed. He was making fun of her. To this man, women were likely no more than sex objects. He most certainly wouldn't be able to conceive of a professional woman unless she looked like a Sherman tank. RoseEllen knew his type.

He smiled into her eyes and she returned his smile. She glanced down at his hands. They were large, with long tapered fingers and black curling hairs that covered the knuckles. This man, with his broad shoulders, his powerful build, his sensitive face with the beginnings of a five o'clock shadow even though he had, presumably, shaved before coming, might be a shade too hirsute. But in spite of a conscious wish to feel otherwise, even minor flaws in his looks appealed to her. There was something unattractive about absolute physical perfection.

"I mean I'm a psychologist," she insisted.

"You?" Disbelief and then amusement welled in his eyes. "Are you a sex therapist?" he asked fliply.

"A family therapist, though I do a lot of individual and group therapy also. I'm in private practice."

"I'd better be careful what I say around you then. Or you'll be pulling out those inkblots. I may as well tell you now that they all look like dancing girls to me."

12

"Perhaps we'd better do word associations then," RoseEllen flung out audaciously. "Jonathan-outdated-male-chauvinist-pig. Nice-to-have-met-you. Good-bye." She stood up.

With a gentle hand he pulled her back into her seat. "I can word-associate better than that. I'll show you how it's done. RoseEllen-run-risk-red-rose-rather-be making love to you than be hanging around this stuffy party."

RoseEllen's eyes blazed with shock and outrage. What unmitigated gall this man had!

Jonathan Wood clasped his hands behind his neck, stretched his long legs in front of him, and studied the features of her face, which had shifted from cool composure to heated indignation. "You sparkle when you're mad. It brings color to those alabaster cheeks and lights to those jade eyes of yours."

"Did you want to get me mad?" she challenged him.

"Not at first. But you're so easy to rile. Does that mean I'm crazy?" He chuckled.

"I doubt it. To paraphrase Freud, if you can work somehow and love somehow you're okay."

"I'm very good at both." He smiled. "You really are beautiful." He looked at her intently.

"I know very well that I'm attractive," she answered with a coolness she didn't feel, "but beautiful I'm not. So save your breath. I should have told you the first time you said it that I don't succumb to flattery."

Jonathan let out a low whistle. "So that's where you're at. First of all, I never say what I don't believe. Hell, you could let your hair flow free and you might even wear a little more makeup, but to the connoisseur champagne is champagne however it's bottled. I know value when I see it—whether it's used cars, abandoned buildings, junk, or women."

"If the champagne is in a Mountain Dew bottle the chances are it's Mountain Dew," she rejoined dryly. She didn't doubt that he was telling the truth about at least one thing, that he was a connoisseur. A man like him would have women crawling out of the woodwork, dazzled by handsomeness and easy charm.

"You're not married." He looked at RoseEllen's ring finger. "Involved?"

"With my career," she clipped.

"It's that important to you, is it? Well," he stated flatly, "I have very little use for psychology or most shrinks." He grinned audaciously. "Psychology is fine for people who can't cope with their lives and have to blame their problems on Mommy or Daddy, but it's not for me. I'm captain of my own ship and I don't need empty words and silly distinctions."

"You must be a genius to have so neatly summed up the whole field of psychology. So much for Freud in two sentences." She looked at the man seated across from her with what she hoped was a detached coolness. There was something about the shrewd sparkle in his dark eyes, the wide, intelligent brow, and the penetrating gaze that conflicted with the rough image he was projecting.

"Not a genius. But I know what I am and what I want."

"Good for you, but not everybody is so fortunate," she answered defensively.

"Why aren't you married?" he persisted. "Don't you like men?"

Startled, RoseEllen gasped. Her voice was icy. "I like gentlemen, a species of which you are clearly not a member." She rose again, and again his restraining hand was on her arm.

"I know about gentlemen. They prefer blondes. Junkmen prefer brunettes. Anyway, gentlemen are out of style. So is the word 'no'."

"Well then, perhaps you'll let this hopeless anachronism go!" Her voice was getting shrill. She noticed people looking at them with interest. To avoid a scene, she sat down.

"Let me tell you about a dream I had." He was smiling tauntingly.

"If you want to talk about dreams you can call my office for an appointment."

He was undaunted. "I dreamt I saw a repressed, frustrated angel in a golden mirror. I fulfilled her fantasies and unleashed her passions. She was tall as far as angels go and slender, maybe too slender. She had a prudish manner about her—the way she pressed her lips together like a stern old schoolmarm." He imitated RoseEllen. "But she had a wide, sensuous mouth that yearned for kisses, cheekbones she must have gotten from a Slavic grandmother, and breasts like pomegranates. She—"

"Why are you doing this?" RoseEllen snapped. "If this is your idea of a seduction it's not very effective."

"But it *is* fun." He chuckled. "You do fascinate me, you know. You don't seem like a psychologist."

"Why not?"

"Let's not talk about that again." He laughed. "How did you ever get into it?"

"People have always interested me and I want to help them. When I took psychology in college I knew that was it. I couldn't stop reading." RoseEllen stopped in midthought. Why, after the outrageous things he had said to

15

her, was she talking to him? She looked down and scrutinized his hands again. They reminded her more of a pianist's hands than a junkman's. There was no dirt under the nails nor calluses which she could see. "You don't seem like a junkman."

"I checked my bundles when I came in," he laughed. "I'm going to close a deal on a truckload of old washing machines right after the party."

She didn't know whether he was teasing her or not. Probably not, she decided.

"How did you get invited here, or are you a gate crasher?" RoseEllen asked mischievously.

"Without my help old Riley wouldn't have opened his clinic. But that's confidential business. I suspect, however, that you're itching to ask the story of my life. Since you haven't asked, I'll tell you. It all started when I was sixteen, with no money for a movie or a date. A classic case. Poor family, et cetera. Anyway, this sixteen-year-old liked tinkering around with old cars. It got him rides and made him friends. He got pretty good at it and wound up owning his own transmission rebuilding business by the time he was twenty-one. From there he went on to auto wrecking and made it big. The rest is history."

"How admirable. It's the American dream."

"There are a few tawdry details," he added impishly.

From his manner, from the way he seemed to dominate his space, from a certain hint of ruthlessness she glimpsed in his face, RoseEllen didn't doubt that there was more than a little bit of tawdriness to the story of his life. She didn't think she cared to pursue the subject. Her own life was as pure as unbleached flour, and sometimes she thought it was as uninteresting. But hers was a healthy life. Undoubtedly, it was healthy. No drugs, very little

16

drinking, no bad influences. She had always kept a tight rein on her emotions. No angry outbursts for her when things didn't go her way, no crying jags, no great big belly laughs, no uncontrollable urges for pizza in the middle of the night, no affairs that made her want to write her love in skywriting from a rented plane. RoseEllen had always been in control. She didn't know why she was that way. It was enough that she was. Judging from her patients, some of whom had no direction in their lives, and for whom she had tremendous empathy, she was very, very lucky. She had always worked hard, and now, with the hefty fees she was commanding and the respect she was garnering from colleagues, she was reaping her just rewards.

The band, which had paused for a break, struck up an old tune. It was one of those torch songs from the early days of Technicolor movies where the heroine, wearing a white, strapless evening gown, would be dallying with the hero on the balcony of an Italian palazzo with a full moon overhead providing the backdrop.

"Shall we dance?" Jonathan asked smoothly.

"I'd rather not," she responded with an outward poise she did not feel.

Annoyance flashed across his features. With hooded eyes he searched her face intently. "Let's dance anyway." He stood up with his hand held out to her.

Irritation was mounting rapidly in her gut. Unused to having her wishes so blatantly disregarded, she didn't quite know how to handle the situation. Should she get up and flounce away? Should she berate him, insult him, freeze him with cold disdain? Her decision was made for her when her hosts, Dr. and Mrs. Riley, approached their table, faces wreathed in smiles.

"Hello, Jonathan, Rosey."

RoseEllen winced. Nobody except Dr. Riley had called her Rosey since she had left adolescence and Clearasil behind. Dr. Riley was a short, balding dynamo of a man with a paternalistic air about him. He had been director of the clinic where she had interned and, much impressed with her work, was now a major source of patient referrals. RoseEllen had the feeling that she would be handling much of the outpatient overflow from his new clinic as well.

She flashed him and his wife a heartfelt smile.

"So you two have met," Dr. Riley said approvingly. "That's nice, very nice. Well, apparently you're getting ready to dance. We'll talk later."

"Don't forget to taste the poached salmon," Mrs. Riley added. "It's divine. Enjoy your dancing. I do so love to watch young people dance."

"That's quite all right," RoseEllen broke in hastily. "We weren't—"

"Mrs. Riley, Doctor." Jonathan nodded respectfully as he held his arm out to RoseEllen.

Under the beaming eyes of the elderly couple, RoseEllen had no recourse but to take it. She felt the hard bulge of muscle under his jacket.

Glowering, she rasped, "That was taking unfair advantage!"

"How do you think I got where I am in the world?" he asked rhetorically. Expertly he guided her onto the dance floor. Though RoseEllen was tall, her chin just came up to his shoulder. With his hand lightly on her back he led her in flowing, whirling movements. RoseEllen hadn't danced for a long time, but under the fluid direction of his body she felt that she could execute the most intricate of

18

steps. The soothing strains of the music and the forceful-
ness of their movement dissipated her anger, and in its
place was a state of heightened sensation. The skin on her
back tingled where his hand rested. When he pressed her
close against the hard wall of his chest she could feel their
hearts beating against each other. Her breasts were flattened against him and she wondered momentarily how
that felt to him. Then all thoughts were suspended and she
closed her eyes. With his hand he pushed her head down
on his shoulder. The music became slower, dreamier, and
he held her even closer. Their movements became un-
dulating and the long, steellike feel of his thighs between,
against, beside hers made goosebumps stand up on her
arms. She hoped that he wouldn't notice. Their hips rolled
together with exquisite timing and she felt the swell of his
desire pressing against her. Loosening his hold on her, he
pulled back slightly. She felt an unexpected sense of disappointment abate when his lips brushed her hair. She heard
his sharp intake of breath and felt its hot caress on her
cheek. When the music ended and a fast number began
they separated. Through glazed eyes, RoseEllen saw that
he was watching her. A small, smug smile played around
the corners of his mouth.

With a muttered apology RoseEllen beat a hasty retreat
to the powder room. The large gold-and-black lounge was
empty save for an attendant. Not even pausing to check
her hair or lipstick, RoseEllen collapsed in a damask-
covered chair. She could feel herself trembling. What was
going on here? She had met a man, a man who could not
be more ill suited to her, a man who was arrogant and
contemptuous, a man who openly decried her profession.
Yet a man undeniably attractive. RoseEllen had a plan for
her life. It included marriage at some distant point in the

future, probably to a colleague with whom she could share case loads and histories. Her life was well ordered and right now it centered upon achievement. Sometimes she felt a pang of loneliness—more like a ping, she would say as she laughed it away. Holidays and Sundays were the hardest, but no one's life, she would think, was guaranteed to be one hundred percent perfect. She was luckier than most, for she had lots of friends who liked and respected her. She had a sterling reputation and she was on a winning streak. Jonathan Wood was a rake and most assuredly disreputable. Better to put him out of her mind. She could not afford any mistakes.

"You okay? Need anything, miss?" the attendant asked solicitously.

Rousing herself, RoseEllen assured her that she was all right. She hastily patted her hair and left two quarters on the discreetly placed glass tray on the counter.

Back in the fray, RoseEllen was almost immediately accosted by Dr. Riley.

"Interesting fellow, that Wood, hmm?"

"Yes, he's interesting," RoseEllen answered with a barely detectable wryness.

"Listen, Rosey, I've been meaning to talk to you all week. Judge McIntyre over there"—Riley indicated a flaxen-haired old gentleman with matching mustache, ruddy cheeks, and aromatic cigar that wafted over half the hall—"has asked me to work with him on a program for driving offenders. I told him I didn't have the time but recommended you for the job. What do you say?"

"Not knowing the details I can't say," RoseEllen answered, "but I'd be glad to go over it with him sometime."

"Good. Let me introduce you." He took RoseEllen's

elbow in a courtly, continental fashion and led her over to the judge's group, which was engaged in raucous laughter.

"Judge, I'd like you to meet Ms. Robbins, the therapist I was telling you about."

A pall fell over the group, initiated by the judge, who cleared his throat at length before answering.

"Miss Robbins," the judge said stiffly as he peered at her, "you're younger than I expected . . . though Dr. Riley here seems to think rather well of you."

"I plead innocence as far as my age is concerned, Your Honor." She paused mischievously to allow the import of her double entendre to sink in. "But I did play an active role in getting any and all recommendations."

One or two of the other men smiled politely.

The judge cleared his throat again and chewed on his cigar before speaking.

"I'll have the plans sent to your office then, and we'll be in touch." He nodded dismissively.

"Very good, sir." RoseEllen smiled as she wandered away, having come to the conclusion that the judge was acutely ill at ease with women. Small talk wouldn't be his strong suit. He was a "good ol' boy" who had yet to be told about "good ol' girls."

Scanning the room guardedly, RoseEllen checked to make sure Jonathan was not lying in wait for her. Her watch said ten thirty. If she could avoid him for another hour she could decently take her leave. In a moment of amused lucidity she thought that he could possibly be avoiding her too. After all, if he had played the satyr she had played the shrew. She spotted him safely ensconsed in the middle of a bevy of young women. Safe enough, she thought. Drifting casually from group to group, laughing at the appropriate times, RoseEllen nonetheless thought of herself as a trapped animal whose capture by a hungry predator was only a matter of time. She didn't know why she felt that way. What had passed between them was probably nothing more than harmless party banter. And a dance. And *what* a dance, her mind chided.

She looked straight ahead, into the mirrored wall, and for the second time that night she saw him staring at her and for the second time that night their eyes locked. Disoriented by the mirrors, startled by the glass prison, her heart catapulted. Like Alice in *Through the Looking-Glass*, she felt herself falling, falling, falling, and the shards of common sense which she tried to grasp slipped away. With her whole body she turned. He wasn't in back of her; he wasn't to the side. For one crazy moment she felt that the mirror was a real place which he, with his compelling maleness, inhabited. And then she saw him walking toward her. If she could have taken flight she would have. Instead she stood still, a forced smile pasted on her face.

"Hello again!" she called brightly.

"Again," he echoed with a meaningful lilt to his voice. "Dance?"

"I'm a little tired."

"Then we'll sit this one out." He motioned to a plum velvet settee nearby. As if she had no will of her own, she acquiesced. *What a therapist I am,* she thought darkly. *Maybe I'd better sign up for my own course in assertiveness training!* She noticed the envious glances of a few of the women as she and Jonathan sat together. It was his physical presence that made him stand out so. The other men, with their florid faces and flaccid bodies, could no more hold a candle to him with his dark, hard, menacing looks than an overly plump housecat could to a sleek panther.

"So tell me, Doc, how do your male patients feel about spilling out their fantasies to you?"

"At ease, I hope."

"Doesn't it get a little"—he paused—"uncomfortable?"

"What are you saying?"

"I would think it a tense situation—talking about sex all the time."

RoseEllen laughed. Even with his sophisticated veneer his interests were as prurient as any callow youth's. "Despite the folklore there's more to psychology than phallic symbols and wombs. Psychologists don't *always* think about sex!"

"Junkmen do."

With her breath caught in her throat she looked down, away from his eyes that seemed to burn, probe, and search into the depths of her soul.

"You should work that out," she said coolly.

"I was planning on it." He grinned wickedly.

Pointedly looking at her watch RoseEllen picked up her silver leather evening pouch.

"I'll be saying my good-byes now. It's been a long day."

"I'll walk you to your car," he offered gallantly.

"That won't be necessary."

"But a pleasure."

With Jonathan beside her RoseEllen thanked her hosts.

"Is Jonathan taking you home? That's nice. It doesn't do for young women to be out alone at night. Not with what this world is coming to," Mrs. Riley opined.

RoseEllen wanted to wipe the Cheshire smile off Jonathan's face. She wanted to inform Mrs. Riley that if she had anything to fear it was only from her protector. She laughed noncommittally.

23

"Nice people, the Rileys," Jonathan started conversationally as he walked with her to the door.

"Uh huh," she uttered grudgingly. "I'd really rather see myself out."

Jonathan lifted one shoulder in a gesture of indifference, though she noticed that his eyes narrowed dubiously. This man wasn't as sure of himself as he pretended, she thought with smug satisfaction. However, he stayed doggedly at her side.

The cool night air slapped against her cheeks and her bare shoulders, making her shiver involuntarily.

"Cold?" He laid an arm lightly around her.

She wriggled out from under his hold.

"Would you rather I take my jacket off for you?" he asked, undaunted. "Or lay it across a puddle, if I can find one?"

"I'd rather you kept it on and let me shiver," she retorted grimly.

Stopping at the cream-colored Volvo she had bought as soon as she was able to convince the finance company that her first month's income was not a fluke, and which, because of the vagaries of big-city traffic, she drove only on weekends, she fished in her purse for the key.

"Why do I have the distinct impression that your personality is not always so grating?" he asked with an irreverent smile.

"I adjust my personality to the situation," she answered in honeyed tones. "And when an untempered male has made his dishonorable intentions as plain as you have, nothing less than 'grating' is deserved."

"I didn't think I came across quite so badly," he apologized in a satiny voice, "but I do believe in keeping my promises, stated openly . . . or insinuated."

24

Before she knew what was happening he had pulled her to him in a strong embrace. His lips were on hers in a forceful, demanding, devouring kiss that more than fulfilled any insinuated promises. RoseEllen gasped in outrage. He took the opportunity to seize her open mouth as a warrior seizes territory that he has conquered. With his insistent tongue he plundered, explored, delighted in the warm, pliant recesses of her mouth. Her hands balled in tight fists, RoseEllen pummeled his back until, with a strangulated whimper, she realized that this had been inevitable. Her fingers fanned out over his broad back and suddenly she stopped fighting. Voluntarily, she yielded her mouth to him, even answering his kisses. Tentatively and then with increasing abandon she darted her tongue into the cavernous depths of his mouth, reveling in the taste, the feel of him. A slow fire had started deep inside her and it blazed now out of control. It had been a long time, she thought, since she had abandoned herself to the pure sensous pleasure of a man's kiss. With his thumb he stroked the corners of her mouth and with half-closed eyes she insisted to herself that no woman would be immune to the masterliness of his technique. His lips moved from the sweet delights of her mouth to shower hot kisses on her face, her neck, the tender lobes of her ears. She leaned back, allowing him freer access to the hollow at the base of her throat. He had not intimately touched her, yet RoseEllen felt the nipples of her breasts straining against the thin fabric of her dress.

"Will you come home with me?" he rasped thickly.

A cloud seemed to lift and RoseEllen pushed him away. She was dangerously close to the point of no return.

"I can't," she whispered hoarsely. "No, I can't."

Half blinded by the tears which had welled unbidden in her eyes, she pulled her car door open, jumped behind the wheel, and pulled away with a roar. She didn't even look in her rear-view mirror.

# CHAPTER TWO

"I'm a middle-aged man
And not one bit ashamed
In thinking that I'm successful
Without a nickel to my name.

"I never have gone hungry
And have always had good health
Have traveled and enjoyed my life
And had no need for wealth."

RoseEllen felt a flood of affection for her balding, rotund
client as he proudly read his latest poems to her. Having
come to her five months ago when she had first opened her
practice, a salesman who couldn't sell and a husband who
didn't know his wife, Pete Mays was a man who kept a
tight lid on his emotions, and RoseEllen had picked up on
that immediately. He was a volcano ready to erupt and
thanks to RoseEllen's skillful therapy, which had often-
times been intense and sometimes painful, the explosion
was creative. The last three sessions had been poetry read-
ings. Pete had never known he had it in him and all the
poetry which had been bottled up somewhere in his subconscious for a half a century came pouring out. He had
decided on a divorce. That was for the best; his sales had
rocketed off his personal chart. RoseEllen smiled and took
a deep breath. She knew what she had to do.

"Pete, I think I've helped you as much as I can, as much

as you needed. You're a confident, aggressive man now and you'll go as far as you want."

"No longer the basket case I was when I walked in here?" He grinned ruefully.

"I would never have called you a basket case." She smiled. "Far from it. You don't need my services anymore."

There was silence. RoseEllen felt little beads of sweat standing out on her forehead. She had made a definite commitment to Pete, as she did with each of her patients, and she had never terminated a client before. But she knew that a good therapist, like a good parent, had to let go when the time was right.

"I'm not ready," Pete said at last.

"Of course you are! Why here you are paying me to listen to those marvelous poems when I should be the one paying you!" she kidded him gently.

"Do you really like them?"

"You bet. And I'd like an autographed copy of the *Collected Works* when you get them ready."

Pete's large head reddened, starting at the ears and spreading simultaneously upward and down. His shiny pink pate looked suspiciously like an off-color bowling ball.

"Well, sure. You'll get the first copy," Pete sputtered. "So you think I can make it on my own, do you? Maybe I can, maybe I can." He paused. "Aggressive, confident, eh? Yeah, I guess that's right." He paused again, as he reached for his misshapen fedora that was at least twenty years out of style. "Thanks, Miss Robbins, for everything." As he started to stand he seemed to hesitate, and then smiled a tight smile as if plucking up his courage.

28

"I'm going to the Pancake House. Care to join me for some waffles?"

"Thanks, but," she patted her flat stomach, "I'm watching my weight." She smiled kindly. "You go ahead and enjoy. You're a good man."

Pete Mays caught the dismissive tone to her voice, and donning his hat, he shuffled out the door, his back straight. "I'll leave the last check with your secretary."

Nodding, RoseEllen sat still for a moment in her soft leather swivel chair. She faced a large potted palm and thought that hers was a bittersweet profession, for with every success came a slight sense of loss.

Her next client was a first timer and the direct result of her introduction to Judge McIntyre at the Riley affair last week. The driving safety program was the judge's baby and he had lost no time in filling RoseEllen in on the details and in sending her the first prospect for rehabilitation. With its emphasis on deconditioning and behavior modification, its preprogrammed texts and gory filmstrips, RoseEllen felt that the program was psychology at its primitive worst, but considering the weightiness of its sponsor and her standing as a newcomer in the field, RoseEllen felt that she had little choice but to agree to use it.

In the first session RoseEllen introduced the program to the young man facing her, gave him a variety of psychological tests, talked with him and tried to assess his mental health. If he were psychotic he was out of the program immediately; if neurotic or simply immature he had a good shot at rehabilitation. When the fifty-minute session came to a close RoseEllen was grateful.

RoseEllen buzzed her secretary. "What's on next, Wilson?"

"Your two o'clock and three o'clocks cancelled for today. I rescheduled them for next week. Wait a minute. I'll be right in."

The door flew open and Wilson Beck, her secretary, sailed in the office. Wilson, twentyish, was an aspiring actor fresh from the too-stiff competition of New York who had honed his secretarial skills until his big break came on Walnut Street in Philadelphia. He typed seventy words a minute, took shorthand with admirable accuracy, and was pretty in that slightly decadent way of blond young men who smoked too much, chased after too many girls, and spent too much time blow-drying their hair. After having interviewed two dozen qualified candidates for the position RoseEllen had chosen Wilson, not only because he had impressed her with his willingness to work hard, but also, she had admitted to herself, because the idea of having a male secretary was too hard to resist.

"Miss Robbins," Wilson began unsteadily, "I know you don't have any regular time slots open for new patients right now, unless you want to start in the late afternoon, but I got a call this morning from a fellow who insisted, but *insisted*, that he had to see you today."

"Who was he referred by?"

"That's just it. He wouldn't say."

RoseEllen tapped her fingers on her desk.

"I gave him eleven o'clock since you had the opening." Wilson's voice was wary. He knew psychologists didn't normally have people walk in off the street. Almost all patients were referrals, either from clinics, city agencies, or other therapists. Signing up for therapy was not, after all, like buying a pair of socks. "He said he was desperate and you were the only one who could help him."

"All right," RoseEllen said wearily. Those patients who

endowed their therapists with superhuman powers were often the most difficult to treat, for they expected that with the wave of a magic wand all their problems would disappear. "What's the fellow's name?"

"A Mr. Wynn. In fact I think I just heard the door opening. That must be him now. I'll have him fill out the forms and bring him on in."

RoseEllen sat immobile in her chair. Her bones felt stiff, for it had been a trying week and she sorely felt the need for some exercise. Her running shoes sat waiting for her in the corner of her office. When she was through with Mr. Wynn she would go for a nice, long run along the East River Drive and start her week's vacation off right, invigorated yet relaxed. She was glad it was Friday and she had nine uninterrupted vacation days ahead of her, except for one small talk she would give at a meeting. Most of this holiday was going to be spent at home doing things she had put off for too long, like repainting her apartment, sorting her clothes, and wrapping her nails (something she had read about but never done).

For reasons she didn't fully understand, everything had annoyed her this past week. When she hadn't been able to open a tin of sardines because she'd inserted the key the wrong way, instead of using a can opener or screw driver, she had, in disgust, thrown the can in her red trash can and was forced to spend the next half hour wiping up the viscous olive oil as it dripped over the sides of the can and into the cracks between the floor tiles. Apparently she hadn't done the best of cleaning jobs, for twice after that she slipped on the spot where the oil had spilled. When her VISA bill was in error, instead of writing the reasonable letter with receipts which common sense dictated, she had called to yell at the computer. And when the washing

31

machine at the corner Laundromat ruined her best cotton knit shirt, the one in dusty pink that made her feel chic and gorgeous, she had cried. She knew the label said HAND WASH ONLY but she was out of Woolite and anyway the stopper in her sink leaked. All in all it was a terrible week. And it had started the morning after that wretched party. Or maybe that night. She wasn't sure.

Her office door opened and Wilson entered, followed by the new client.

"Mr. Wynn," Wilson announced as he walked out backward through the open door, making sure it clicked behind him.

Her eyes dilated from fury, RoseEllen glared at the man who seated himself blithely across from her. "So it's Mr. Wynn, is it?" she hissed through clenched teeth.

Jonathan grinned. "You do what you have to in this world. Had I followed conventional wisdom and called you up for a date you would have refused."

"It looks like you won for now, Mr. Wynn. Here we are face to face. You might as well take a good look because it's the last one you're likely to get."

"By my watch I've got forty-five minutes to go," he answered nonchalantly.

"Did it ever occur to you that I might not appreciate your barging in like this?" she demanded.

"Hey, I'm paying fifty smackeroos for the pleasure of sitting here, so I'd like to get my money's worth."

"No fee."

"I've already paid."

"Wilson will refund your money," RoseEllen countered, trying to control her anger.

"No thanks. So"—Jonathan looked around the spacious office with its decorously situated plants, framed museum prints, and overflowing bookcases—"what do you do around here for R and R?"

"Cut out paper dolls, what else?" RoseEllen retorted dryly.

Jonathan raised one charmingly cockeyed brow in a way that reminded her of a naughty fox terrier.

She tapped her foot impatiently. "If you wanted to see me so badly you should have called in any case, the way a *normal* person would have."

"Actually, I did try. But all I got was your recording device and I'll be hanged before I talk to a machine instead of a woman! Where do you spend all your time anyway?"

He was probably telling the truth, RoseEllen mused, softening. There had been more than the normal number of clicks on her machine. Those people who refused to leave messages on the device were legion, far outnumbering the ones who did. It was all so frustrating hearing those clicks and thinking that maybe she had missed the one call that would change her life (someone leaving her a million dollars or a committee naming her therapist of the year) that she was thinking about getting rid of the device altogether. For some reason she had seen three movies last week after work, visited four shopping malls, and badgered friends and family with unannounced evening visits. Usually she enjoyed quiet evenings at home, but not last week. Last week she didn't want to be alone and unoccupied, except when she was sleeping.

She shrugged ungraciously.

"Don't you want to reveal your secrets?" he prodded.

"If you have to know," she teased, "I was scouting alleys, rounding up a fair number of junkmen and giving them all lobotomies!—at least those who hadn't yet had one."

"I see I'll have to watch my step around you, Dr. Jekyll. Why so nasty—or is it all a defense?"

RoseEllen blanched, for truthfully she didn't know. Though she wasn't exactly another Miss Manners, she couldn't recall the last time she had been so purposefully rude.

Jonathan raised his eyebrows. She had the uncomfortable feeling that he knew what she was thinking. Reaching over to her desk he picked up a booklet.

"Pennsylvania State Drivers' Manual," he read. "Is this your version of escapist reading?"

"Not exactly. I use it in a driver safety program I'm involved with. In fact, the initiator of the program made contact with me at the Riley party last week."

"So the party wasn't a total loss," Jonathan bantered as he absentmindedly leafed through the manual. "One thing's for sure. This will never make the best seller list. I remember only too well studying this thing." He deadpanned, "If you're traveling at fifty miles an hour and the car ahead is traveling forty you'll need about ten seconds to pass. During this time you'll travel six hundred and two feet, which is exactly thirty-six car lengths. However, if the vehicle in front of you is a tractor-trailer you might travel fifty-one car lengths while passing at fifty miles an hour. And if you're like most people you need a calculator to do the math so you're rifling in your glove compartment for the pocket calculator you got as a free gift from the bank and you don't notice the motorcycle that's creeping up on your left or the Mercedes that passed the truck on your right and when you finally figure out that you need four seconds at fifty miles an hour to pass you ram into the cycle, knock the Mercedes onto the shoulder and cause a twenty-five vehicle smackup. Then you wind up in the slammer for involuntary manslaughter with a copy of the state drivers' manual to keep you company!"

Despite herself RoseEllen found that she was laughing. "Somehow I can't imagine you ever having that problem. I'll bet you're a fairly competent driver."

"I am," he winked conspiratorially.

"On the other hand," RoseEllen continued, "it wouldn't surprise me if you drove too fast."

"Very insightful. I like living life in the fast lane."

"Simply out of professional curiosity, how does it make you feel when you speed?"

"Like a *real man,*" he answered facetiously. "How does it make you feel when you fight against an overwhelming passion?"

"I wouldn't know," she answered coldly.

He brought his arms from behind his neck up over his head and stretched. RoseEllen could see the muscles of his shoulders bulging through the tapered shirt that was rolled up as high as his elbows to reveal thick, sinewy forearms. He seemed to dominate the office, no mean trick in surroundings geared to give the therapist the illusion of power. RoseEllen's oak desk dwarfed the rest of the furniture and her leather swivel chair matched it in proportion. By contrast, Jonathan's Eames style chair was not meant for a man taller than six feet two.

His lips twitched as, with what she considered a look of insufferable arrogance, he caught her studying him.

"Has anybody told you what kissable lips you have?"

"No."

"They probably wouldn't have dared." He chuckled. "Kissable lips but thunderclouds for eyes."

She gritted her teeth and silently cursed fate that had

sent Jonathan Wood to the party that night and here today.

"I can hardly believe that you came here to dissect the features of my face." Exasperation was plain in her voice. "Nor to beg a kiss if that's what you're getting at! I may as well tell you right now that I never kiss patients, real or pretend!" she mocked.

"Why not? Even your precious Freud kissed a patient or two on occasion."

"How would you know?" she demanded icily.

"Even junkmen can read! Enough of this game. We're not here as therapist and patient."

"We're not here as Romeo and Juliet either. We wouldn't be here at all if you hadn't used the most infantile chicanery on my secretary."

"I couldn't help myself." He grinned winningly. "I'm bewitched."

"Oh, come on." She laughed, her voice softening. "I've been anything but bewitching. Witchy, maybe." To cover up the confusion which descended upon her, she jumped up and strode over to the film projector, where she started rewinding the filmstrip she had shown during the previous session. Having always felt that she had a mechanical IQ of a moron she realized she had chosen the wrong activity to divert attention from herself. She would have been more successful if she had stood on her head!

"Need any help?"

"No, thanks. I can manage," she replied offhandedly as she fumbled with the machine. She felt herself redden as her first attempt to rewind the filmstrip became her second and only succeeded with her third. She was thankful that Jonathan spared her any witty commentary on her performance.

"Do you have any more appointments today?" Jonathan asked.

"You're the last one." She grinned. "And a hard act to follow."

"Then you can come out with me. We'll take a long walk along South Street, look in the antique shops, and work up a healthy appetite for dinner at Le Bec Fin. They make superb sweetbreads."

"I've never been to Le Bec Fin. Couldn't afford it. And I don't care what kind of junkman you are, no junkman's earnings are enough to blow on a dinner there!" RoseEllen didn't understand the reason for her outburst. Why should she care what he did with his money?

Jonathan's eyes twinkled mischievously. "How about Horn and Hardart's then?" He named the vintage Philadelphia cafeteria. "Their baked beans are unbeatable."

"I appreciate the offer but I can't," RoseEllen refused politely.

"Why not? Even roses wilt if they're not nourished."

"I have plans."

"With someone?" he asked offhandedly.

"By myself, though I can't see that it makes any difference." She pronounced the words slowly, as if it were an effort to speak. In a way it was. It would be easy to let this man sweep her along and possibly quite pleasant, almost like riding into a giant water flume. But at the end of the flume there was always the great splash into icy waters.

"Well then, my ploy seems not to have worked. I don't win." There was a satirical note beneath the surface dejection of his voice. His eyes searched her face and then swung away over her office, stopping at the corner of the office near a narrow mahogany wardrobe. A pair of Adidas running shoes stood almost hidden in its shadow.

When he stood to leave, he did his best to assume a somber expression. "Good-bye, RoseEllen. I've got to run now." He closed the door softly.

That she had already practically memorized the intricate framed poster of Chinese snuff bottles did not stop her from sitting in her office for a long time just staring at it. The various shapes and colors of the design calmed her and stopped her wayward mind from racing along a dangerous course. She sighed.

# CHAPTER THREE

RoseEllen started her five-mile run at boathouse row, a series of Victorian structures built of rich purple stone which served as boating clubs. Along with hundreds of other runners and bicyclists she followed the banks of the Schuylkill River. The route, dotted with sculptures and fountains, hot dog vendors and lovers, provided a plethora of sight and sound. So immersed in all that was going on—especially in the efforts of the college boating crews whose young men heaved and hoed as if their lives depended on it—RoseEllen found that she would occasionally lose her stride. She concentrated now on improving her time. She ran a ten-minute mile. Her goal was seven minutes.

Her legs were beginning to ache as she pushed herself harder. Her breathing was heavy, her lungs felt as if they were on fire, and sweat stood in little beads on the bridge of her nose. There was a price to pay for having a sedentary job. That she walked ten blocks to and from her office was not, it seemed, going to make Olympic material out of her. As she willed her legs to move faster she began to think of her body as a machine, a machine that needed oil, perhaps, but that was still in working order. All that was necessary was self-discipline and willpower.

The sound of footsteps thudding on the pavement behind her disturbed her concentration. That the runner's stride sounded like a pounding in her ears was due more to the heightened sensitivity which physical exertion sometimes produced than to reality, for she knew that the runner behind landed lightly. But why didn't he pass, whoever he was? Obligingly she slowed her pace. Nobody passed, yet the pounding behind remained constant. She bit her lip in vexation. Why couldn't that blasted person leave a courteous distance between them? There were unwritten rules of conduct for runners and number one was to avoid intruding on someone else's territory. She increased her speed. The pace of the runner behind quickened. She decreased her speed again. The footsteps drummed to a slower beat. From annoyance fear was born. Was her would-be escort bent on harassing her? Perhaps he was a mugger or a rapist! Broad daylight and a public place provided little protection against the criminal who doggedly pursued his victim. Thankfully she recalled the twenty-dollar bill she had stuffed into her back pocket and prayed that it would be enough to thwart a mugger's wrath. Suddenly the footsteps seemed to gather speed, and she prepared to ward off an attack.

"Don't speed. It's against the law! And you might wind up in therapy!" a figure in white designer jogging togs tossed at her as he passed easily to disappear in a blur behind a clump of trees ahead.

"Jonathan Wood!" RoseEllen's mouth fell open as she followed the same shady path as he. Would he never leave her alone?

"Great day for a run," he commented as he came up beside her from under the mimosa where he had been running in place.

"I *was* enjoying it," RoseEllen sniffed.

"There's nothing like fresh air and beautiful scenery. It clears the mind. Any objection to my running along with you?"

"Would it matter?" she panted.

Jonathan grinned. His running seemed effortless. For all his apparent exertion he could have been playing Scrabble. RoseEllen knew her own face was red and feared her eyes were bulging.

"That's a nice running outfit you have. The junk business must be good," she taunted.

"Couldn't be better. I like your cutoffs. Even more than the cutoffs I like what's in them. Nice and firm." He gave her a devastating grin.

RoseEllen looked at him as if he were mad.

"And I like your legs. Well-developed calf muscles. I'll bet you took ballet lessons when you were a kid," he added knowingly.

"The only bar I ever held was made of chocolate," she retorted flippy. "How did you find me?"

"Where else would a Philadelphian run but along the East River Drive?" he said matter-of-factly.

"How did you know I was going running? Oh"—she answered her own question—"you saw the shoes. Well, why did you want to find me?"

"Need you ask?"

"What I need to ask is do you always answer a question with one of your own?"

Jonathan laughed as he bounded ahead. "Stick around and you'll find out!"

As she watched him she thought that if anybody had well-developed calf muscles it was he. His body was straight and fleet and anybody looking at him could have taken him for a professional runner. It seemed so effortless. He was a different breed, RoseEllen thought over the pounding of her heart, a different breed altogether. Yet why was she concentrating on the rippling of his muscles as he receded from view, and why this empty feeling when

41

he was gone? Was she developing a masochistic streak? Did she enjoy being insulted and talked to as if she were just another piece of meat on the market? Nice calves indeed!

The balls of her feet were beginning to burn and her legs to rebel against the constant punishment of the hard pavement. She looked at her watch as she passed the four-mile marker. A nine-minute mile! Not too bad, she congratulated herself.

"Keep it up. You're doing great!" Jonathan's voice rang out as he approached her once again.

He must have circled around, RoseEllen thought as she turned her head to stare straight into his eyes.

They ran together in silence, a silence that filled her, forcing her awareness to center on him. She focused upon the curiously pleasant, slightly pungent male smell of him, upon the way his curls lay carelessly tousled, upon the open triangle at his neck where his glistening chest hairs provided the only clue to his exertion. Willing herself to stare straight ahead, she thought that it was all right to appreciate his looks. It was purely from an aesthetic and objective point of view. After all, if she pretended that he looked like every other male of the species she would be fooling herself and then she might really be in trouble. Men liked to look at beautiful women. Women liked to look at handsome men. That was all there was to it.

Up ahead she caught sight of the cluster of small statues that marked the end of her five miles. What a relief. The pain in her legs was becoming unbearable and her lungs felt like they were about to burst. Yet she felt an odd compulsion to keep on running. One more mile and then she would stop. After all, she didn't want this man running so effortlessly beside her to think she had quit on his account. Looking up at him she caught his eyes moving quickly away from her. Hastily she fixed her own glance straight ahead, but not before the strong line of his jaw and the sinewy strength of his neck etched themselves in her memory. A nice physical specimen, she told herself again. With the increased distance the pain in her legs was joined by a heaviness.

"Do you want to rest?" he asked gently.

She nodded.

"Over there." He pointed to a shady, old crab apple tree. They slowed to a walk. Though she was tired, tireder than she had ever been, for she had never run better, she felt exhilarated from the run. Perspiration was streaming down her cheeks in rivulets and the strands of hair which had escaped her bun were stuck to her neck. She did not make a pretty picture, she thought. Jonathan looked as if he had just come back from the corner newstand. His breath was not even slightly ragged. The pupils of his eyes, deep, unfathomable, were ringed with a golden edge that seemed to capture the sunlight. There was a boyish appeal to his smile which she had never noticed.

He stretched out in the long grass as RoseEllen sank to her knees. She stuck the sweet root end of a blade of grass between her teeth.

"Ah," he groaned softly. "There's nothing finer than the sight of blue sky between the leaves of a tree, a good run, good company." He breathed deeply. "Good smells." Rolling over on his side he smiled, a smile that lit up his face. "I like the way you run. You've got good form."

"Thanks. So do you."

"I should. I run every day. It's the greatest antidote for civilization ever invented. It gives me a feeling of freedom;

43

it lets the primitive man out, the one hiding," he stated comically, "behind this urbane veneer."

"As long as you don't start dragging women away by their hair that's great. I know what you mean though. And running also gives me a feeling of absolute control. I set my pace, I set my goal, I set my limit. There's no one to please, no test to pass. And I only have myself to beat. When I finish a run"—she laughed self-consciously—"I feel like I've really accomplished something, sort of pure."

To her surprise Jonathan didn't laugh at that. He nodded as if he understood.

"It's good for what ails you—great for tension. No matter how blue you're feeling a good run will make you feel better. It's like having your own private psychologist with you!" As he finished talking Jonathan took a white handkerchief out of his pocket and gently mopped her brow. "The salt will make your eyes sting," he explained quickly as if to thwart an anticipated rebuff.

She sat still for him. Philadelphia, in the summer, was often sticky. Though Philadelphians often grumbled about the weather it was that very humidity that gave the city its uniquely lush, rain-forest appearance. RoseEllen could feel her T-shirt with its wet patches clinging to her body.

"I wouldn't mind jumping into an ice-cold pool now," she remarked wistfully.

"Excellent suggestion." Standing up, he extended his hand to her.

As she felt his big fingers curl possessively around her small, slender ones, she startled. How could so insignificant, so innocent a contact provide her with so delicious an array of sentiments? She felt warm and attractive and she liked his touch. It made her imagine his hands on her legs, her hips, all over. She shook her head and jumped to her feet.

"Thank you. What did you have in mind? Are you a member of the Philadelphia Athletic Club?"

"Nothing so fancy. Come on." With her hand still enveloped in his they sprinted across the green.

"Think you can make a slow easy run back to the art museum?"

"Sure, why not?" she fibbed.

Pushing herself beyond endurance, she ran. His strides were long and loping, hers short and quick. He led her across the grass rather than along the winding bicycle path on which they had come, cutting their distance considerably.

"Why don't we walk the rest of the way?" she croaked.

One look at her beet-red face and Jonathan slowed to a walk. "Why didn't you say so sooner?"

They walked in companionable silence for which RoseEllen was grateful. She couldn't have found the energy even to utter the cleverest line or comeback. The museum loomed just ahead. They skirted the building and headed for the wide boulevard of flags (Philadelphia's Champs Élysées) along which every nation's banner flew. Stopping abruptly at an ornate Roman fountain Jonathan gestured toward the sparkling spray.

"Who needs a pool?"

Aghast, RoseEllen watched as he peeled off his white shirt and kicked off his suede running shoes.

"You're crazy!"

In response, Jonathan took a running leap and landed with a loud splash in the fountain's lower level. Drops of water rained on her head, in her eyes, and on the steaming sidewalk. Momentarily transfixed by the daring of his act and even more by the sight of him half naked, RoseEllen gulped. Here was a man with a physique of such power and virility, of such superb proportion, that he could make any woman ache with desire. Black curling hairs covered a broad expanse of tanned chest to disappear in a thin line beneath the waistband of his shorts. Muscles bulged in his shoulders, his arms, his back—silent testimony to daily physical exercise. If she were the nestling type, RoseEllen mused, here was a chest she would enjoy nestling against. His shorts were tight against his slim, strong hips, and his legs looked as if they were used to running marathons. A fine physical specimen, she thought again (how many times was it now that she had said that to herself?) in a frantic effort to distance herself from him.

"Come on in. The water's great!" he shouted as he leaned against the equine statue.

She tore her eyes from him. What in the world was wrong with her? It was as if she had never seen a man's body before!

"Are you kidding? You could get arrested for that!"

"For what, molesting a horse?" he jested. "Then you can rehabilitate me."

"Uh uh. Count me out."

"Go ahead, girlie," a panhandler, carrying all his worldly possessions in a brown paper bag, urged. "Yer boyfriend's got the right idea. Got any spare change?"

Taken aback by the request RoseEllen checked her pockets. All she had was the twenty.

"Uh, no. Sorry," she muttered guiltily.

"Here you go, mac." Jonathan was out of the fountain, dripping beside her as he handed the man a bill. "And for you, Miss Robbins, I have something also." Scooping her up in his arms he ran with her to the fountain. At the same time as she was screeching for him to stop, she was conscious of the cold wetness of his hard body.

"Don't you dare! Let me down this minute!"

"Hold your breath," he whispered, allowing his lips to graze her ear.

She shivered just before she felt herself being dumped into the icy pool.

"You're going to be sorry for this!" she sputtered as she came up to look into his laughing face.

"Give her more, mister," two passing youths chortled as they swayed to the music blaring from their briefcase-size radio. "Ya gotta teach that woman her place!"

"Male chauvinism is alive and well in the younger generation too," she said dryly.

"I'm not a male chauvinist," Jonathan protested.

"Oh no? What would you call it?"

"Realistic!" He grinned to show he wasn't serious. "Watch out!" he shouted, and with a slap of his hand on the water, splashed her full in the face.

If there was one thing RoseEllen had learned as a child in rural Pennsylvania, with all the summers spent in the local swimming hole, it was how to splash mean and hard. She put those early lessons to use now and nearly drowned him with a nonstop, torrential barrage of splashing.

"Truce, truce. I surrender!" he gurgled through his laughter. "That'll teach me to mess with a woman!"

"I'm glad to see you're a fast learner," she taunted.

"Come over here and sit with me." He patted the marbled step onto which he had lowered himself.

"I think we'd better get out of this fountain. I'm positive it's illegal to be here—unless you're a pigeon."

"Sit down or I'll dunk you," he menaced with mock gruffness. "Nobody can beat me at dunking."

Rolling her eyes upward she acquiesced. "All right, but only for a minute. What if one of my patients sees me here?"

"They'll find out you're human," he said with a smile that took the sting out of his words.

"You're hard to figure out," RoseEllen said. "Everything you do and say contradicts something else."

"Keep 'em guessing, that's my motto." He grinned.

An elderly woman walked past them with a frown and clucked her tongue.

"Let's go," RoseEllen repeated.

"She's just jealous. Wait a minute. I'll ask her to join us." Jonathan winked. He stood up.

"Incorrigible, that's what you are." She spoke softly.

She, too, stood, glad yet sorry to be leaving. There was something daringly unconventional, almost liberating in so small an act as splashing in a public fountain. Lost in thought, she didn't know how it happened, but suddenly she slipped on the glassy smooth bottom to lurch against Jonathan. He held out a hand to steady her and she didn't know how that happened either but she felt his hand graze her breast. Stiffening, she pulled away. Silence hung heavy between them. RoseEllen didn't know what to do with her eyes. She looked at her feet, which appeared large and wavy under the ripples of the pool and felt, rather than saw, his eyes on her. Her shirt was plastered against her body and her shorts clung to her thighs.

"You're very alluring."

Raising her eyes tentatively she realized that his gaze was focused on the full swell of her breasts. She felt herself blushing as to her horror she watched her nipples, even through the fabric of her shirt, harden and rise. The flimsy

48

bra she wore did little to hide the effect he was having on her.

"And more vulnerable than you let on," he added.

With his hand he tilted her chin upward. Her eyes remained wide with disbelief as his lips brushed hers. It took a few seconds but when she pulled away her voice was rasping. "Don't ever do that again!"

"I get the impression that you like it." His eyes seemed flecked with bits of steel. "You're not nearly so indifferent as you pretend."

She became aware that he was gripping her tightly around the wrists. He pulled her close and deliberately and slowly he lowered his mouth to hers. His lips pressed against her tightly closed ones. With his thumb he stroked the corner of her mouth as his moved to possess her, this time more thoroughly. His kiss was drugging. With his tongue, so velvety and strong, he parted her lips and she, despite all good sense, welcomed him. The uncontrollable fluttering deep inside her was distressing. How easy it was to submit to him.

"Come home with me," he whispered huskily. "My place is just across the street." He pointed to the Philadelphian, one of the city's poshest condominium apartment buildings.

"Just what kind of junk dealer are you?" she asked scornfully, grateful for the respite. "There aren't many people who can afford to live there."

"An impassioned junk dealer—one who wants to touch and look and love at his leisure, one who wants to explore this uncharted territory before him in infinite detail."

"I'm not a territory," she snapped. "Why don't you do your exploring in Wyoming and leave me alone?"

"There's only one way to shut you up," he countered

as he drew her against him to kiss her again. This kiss was brief, playful almost. He straightened and moved away from her almost before she realized that her lips, her tongue, her teeth were answering him in kind.

"You taste so good it makes me hungry."

Not quite sure what hunger he was talking about, RoseEllen waited for him to clarify his statement.

"There's a hot dog wagon over there. Do you want yours with the works?"

She nodded in amazement as if nothing out of the ordinary had passed between them, while he bounded over the side of the fountain to the vendor on the next corner. She stepped gingerly over the slippery marble side, careful not to lose her footing again. Anger shook her. To claim her so soulfully, to make her yield to his kiss and then to abandon her for a hot dog! This was a man who played power games. She was glad he had stopped, because she wanted no part of him. Yet she did not want to be tossed away like a used rag doll, even though, she rebuked herself, she had shown today that she had no more backbone than a rag doll.

Dripping wet, with a puzzled frown on her face, RoseEllen knew she looked strange. Her frown deepened as she spied Jonathan sprinting back, precariously balancing an armload of hot dogs and sodas.

"I'm not hungry," she spat out.

"Sit down." He motioned to one of the benches which dotted the small plaza. "You can keep me company while I eat, then."

Like an automaton, she followed him and he laid the food out on a bench in front of the fountain.

"Have a Coke, at least." The frosty can hissed as he pulled off the aluminum tab. Her lips parched, RoseEllen reached out for the beverage and drank thirstily. "Take a hot dog too. Sabrett's finest, after all." She reached hesitantly for the one with the most mustard and the least saurkraut. The hot dog, sweating in its casing, reminded her of herself.

Jonathan was laughing at her. "I thought you weren't hungry. You're easy, lady."

The hand holding the hot dog posed in mid-air, RoseEllen looked up sharply. "Not as easy as you think."

"Oh yes, and sweet and succulent—once the shell is cracked."

"First I'm a territory and now I'm a crab." She grimaced.

"Or a nut." He laughed. "You only have to get over your fear of me."

"I have no fears," she retorted.

"Not a one?"

"Well, I do have one: a fear of"—she paused dramatically—"butterscotch pudding!"

Jonathan laughed appreciatively. His eyes seemed to darken. "You're so different from other women I've known. A man would have to be very careful to avoid falling in love with you."

RoseEllen felt goosebumps standing out on her arms. She jumped up. "I've got to go now. I think I see my bus."

He laid a restraining hand on her arm. "Don't let me scare you off."

"You have already." She winced.

His eyes twinkled. "I suppose that now I can't invite you up to see my etchings."

"Etchings are passé," she retorted flippantly.

"I should have known a sophisticated lady like you

wouldn't fall for that line. To you I say, how about coming up for a hot shower and a dry pair of shorts?"

She looked at him searchingly. "I'll take the bus—wet."

Raising his eyebrows expressively he let go her arm. As she observed the white spots on her tanned skin left by the pressure of his fingers she saw that he too had noticed them.

"The brute doesn't know his own strength," he muttered apologetically.

"Doesn't he?—My bus!" she pointed. It really was her bus that was coming now, and she started to run. Though she didn't turn around she could feel his eyes, like laser beams, burning into her.

Feeling a cramp on her left side she ran with every last ounce of energy. If she missed the bus she would have a fifteen minute wait for the next one and she knew she wouldn't be waiting alone. The bus was about a block behind her, she thought as she forced her legs to move. Then halfway down the block its shifting gears roared in her ears. Neck to neck with her the bus passed with an impolite belching of exhaust in her face. Her spirits sagged but lifted immediately upon her watching, open-mouthed, as Jonathan sprinted past her to meet the bus at its stop. As she arrived there he was importuning the driver to wait just another half minute.

"Thank you," she panted as she reached in her pocket for the token she always carried.

Sinking gratefully into an empty seat she stared out the window.

Getting up finally at her stop, her moist thighs ripped away from the plastic seat like a Band-Aid from a raw wound, knocking her out of her self-imposed lethargy. Almost of its own accord her body had responded to his playful kisses in the fountain, had indeed yearned for more. No other man—no psychologist, no attorney, no businessman—whom she had dated had ever awakened her like this junkman had in a few minutes of teasing. What on earth was happening here?

# CHAPTER FOUR

RoseEllen put down her mug of coffee after draining it to the dregs. She had drunk three glasses of milk the night before in an effort to fall asleep and had been drinking coffee all morning in an effort to stay awake. This was unlike her and an absolutely horrible state in which to begin her vacation. August was the traditional vacation month for therapists and there was so much that RoseEllen had planned that she didn't want to muck it up with insomnia.

Many of RoseEllen's vacations had been spent at her favorite spot at Cape May on the Jersey shore, with its Victorian gingerbread houses and low-key atmosphere. But in the last couple of years she had discovered Nantucket, the wonderful whaling town off the coast of Massachusetts, and Stockbridge, a small town nestled in the Berkshires that boasted the highest quality theater and concerts in the summertime. Of the last, however, she wasn't quite sure. Some of the people who flocked to Stockbridge, intellectuals and arty types from New York, New Haven, and Boston, who spoke only in four-syllable words, had struck her as a little too impressed with themselves. Perhaps on her next vacation she would return to simpler Cape May. Anyway, she didn't have to decide this summer. With the short time she had she would stay home, doing what had to be done. She would repaint her living room, strip the floor (she knew that under the layers of wax and dirt she would uncover wood eventually), repot the plants which had grown so big she had to lean them against the wall to stand them up, and buy one or two moderately priced antiques for the empty half of her living room.

RoseEllen considered her apartment in center city Philadelphia to be a real find. She had three high-ceilinged rooms with authentic moldings, two stone fireplaces, a bay window scalloped by a wrought iron French terrace, and an authentic stained glass panel over the front door. Her furnishings included a signed nineteenth-century rolltop desk (her graduation present to herself), a handmade braided rug and a patchwork quilt (bought before they became fashionable), lots of wicker, and a round, oak kitchen table graced by a three-hundred-year-old enamel chamber pot containing a bunch of fresh daisies.

Pulling on a pair of faded jeans and an old shirt and wrapping a scarf around her hair, RoseEllen glanced at herself in the mirror. If the hippy look ever came back into style she would be very a la mode! She moved her furniture into the center of the living room, spread newspapers and a drop cloth on her floor, and searched in her odds and ends drawer for a screwdriver to open the first can of paint. She paused, thinking that it might be better if she paid her bills before she started to paint. It would be nice to get them out of the way early, and then she could just put them in a drawer until the first. Her rent, her electric bill, telephone, car loan, a dental bill—she scribbled her name on all those checks, anxious to be done with it. The speed with which her money dribbled away always amazed her. The only checks she didn't mind signing, that she in fact enjoyed writing out, were for an international foster parent plan in which she participated. She had been so touched by the pleading photographs in the plan's promotional literature that she had adopted not one, but four youngsters, making this bill one of each month's more notable payments. She not only felt that it was right and proper for her to share, since she had so much, but more important she wanted to take care of these children. With each check she wrote out she felt an increased sense of responsibility for the children she had "adopted." There was Aruna, the waiflike child from India with the enormous brown eyes. There was Billy, the American Indian who suffered from poor health. There was Luís from Colombia and there was Margaret from a village in Kenya. She exchanged letters and photographs with the children and kept theirs in a special album. She felt proud when one of the children would write her of a success and sad at their misfortunes. She had never told anyone about her "children," not even her own parents. She didn't want to be praised or patted on the head for something she felt was so basic. Sealing the last envelope, she placed it on top of the stack and fastened a rubber band around it. Now she was ready to start working.

She had decided to complete one room at a time, painting and floor stripping. That way only one room at a time would be in a shambles. She decided to start with the living room.

RoseEllen painted efficiently if not expertly with a paintbrush and roller. The creamy tones of the elegant color, French vanilla, fitted the room with its archways and cornices. Having completely forgotten the time she ignored the rumblings of lunchtime hunger and in a fit of compulsiveness finished the first coat. Then she crawled over her rolled up rug to enjoy her reward, a hunk of salami and a Tab. Just then there was a knock at the door.

"Come on in," she called, figuring that it was her downstairs neighbor, who had said she might drop by to check on RoseEllen's progress. Everyone had warned her that with all the detail work she would be making a mistake not to call in a professional to do the job.

"It's not too bad for a first coat, is it?" she gloated, as she chomped on her salami.

"Not bad at all," came the resonant reply, "though it looks like you could do with a helping hand."

"Oh no," she almost choked. "What did I do to deserve this?"

As he crossed the room to where she lay, Jonathan rolled up the sleeves of his polo shirt. "You missed a few spots here"—he pointed—"and there. Those corners are hard to get. Got an extra brush?"

"No," she replied just as he spied her two other new brushes lying on the floor, still in their plastic covers.

"Why do I put up with you?" He grinned as he picked up a brush.

"I certainly never asked you to."

As if pondering that point, Jonathan paused, clicked his tongue, and proceeded to dip his brush into the paint.

"You're not going to paint in that shirt, I hope. I mean, money may come easy to you but a designer shirt is a designer shirt!" RoseEllen exclaimed, horrified.

"I'm beginning to think I bring out your maternal instincts. What I want is to bring out the tigress!" He roared playfully. With a dutiful expression on his face he unbuttoned his shirt and tossed it on a table. "This better?"

Gulping, RoseEllen shrugged and silently berated herself for her big mouth. Why should she care about his shirt anyway? What she wanted was to paint her walls and not be distracted. She stared at his chest with its rippling muscles and rich, curly black hair. Just as there were "leg men" or "hip men," she thought humorously, she was a "chest woman." That's all there was to it. With studied indifference, she swallowed the last of her salami, offered him something to eat, and picked up her own paintbrush. Her back to him, she began to paint the arched entranceway separating her small foyer from the living room. Jonathan, she learned as she glanced out of the corner of her eye, was doing the intricate detail work of the cornices. He was, she had to admit, making himself useful. Detail work was what she disliked, preferring the broad, easy strokes of flat wall painting where she didn't have to think or be careful. Thinking and being careful were things she needed a vacation from.

They didn't talk much while they worked. After a while, RoseEllen put on the stereo.

"Do you like Linda Ronstadt?"

"Does a junkman like junk?" he asked rhetorically.

RoseEllen played the album and thought that, with the sun shining through the stained glass in one of her panes, the sweet strains of Ronstadt's singing, the mindlessly satisfying activity and, yes, the company, there was something almost idyllic about the afternoon.

"You've got French vanilla freckles on your nose." Jonathan laughed.

"Why," RoseEllen asked hesitantly, "are you helping me?"

"I want to. There's more to me than meets the eye."

"What meets the eye isn't so bad." RoseEllen laughed shyly.

"That might be the nicest thing you've ever said to me. Ah, the rewards of perseverence and a good paint job!" he added in jest. "What's next on the agenda? I hope you weren't planning on stripping the floors?"

"Are you a mind reader or do my floors look that bad?"

"I'm a pessimist and floor stripping is the worst of all possible jobs."

"I won't sue if you don't help me. In fact, I wouldn't even let you do it. That's too much to expect or even accept," RoseEllen protested.

"Do you have a beer?" Jonathan asked.

"Sorry. How about a Tab?"

Jonathan looked at her quizzically. "Mind if I take inventory?"

"Help yourself. The refrigerator's in the kitchen."

"In the kitchen? Amazing!" He wiped his brow. "This is impossible," he called from the kitchen, and rattled off the meager contents of her refrigerator. "Tab, diet cream, NoCal cherry, white wine, French label, carrot sticks, frozen quiche, Worcestershire sauce, sprouts, Vichy water, raspberry soup! Can a steak-and-potatoes man ever find love and happiness with a cold fruit soup eater?"

"No," she yelled back with the same mock gravity. "We would be doomed to a life of arguing about restaurants."

As Jonathan gulped a tall glass of tap water, RoseEllen followed him into the kitchen. She could not help but notice the perfect lines of his back. His skin looked like satin, his muscles like steel. His shoulders were broad, his waist narrow, his buttocks through his jeans were sassily masculine. When Jonathan turned around she thought that his eyes flickered knowingly over her face.

"I was just coming in to get the rags," she lamely excused her presence in the kitchen.

"Of course." He moved obligingly from the sink so that she could reach underneath it.

The stripping, RoseEllen mused, was a lot more strenuous and time-consuming than slopping on a first coat of paint had been. First they had to take everything out of the room, making passage to the bedroom virtually impossible. Then Jonathan removed the molding.

"That's one step that never even occurred to me," RoseEllen admitted.

"This way we'll be able to sand all the way to the edge without damaging the baseboards," Jonathan explained.

For all of Jonathan's efforts with the sanding machine RoseEllen could see no discernible difference in the floor. "I heard tell once there's wood down there somewhere," she opined disgustedly.

"How times have changed," Jonathan muttered. "It used to be that a man courted with bouquets of red roses. Today it's done with sandpaper and Sherwin Williams!"

"Is that what you're doing, courting me?"

"Of course." He smirked. "And stripping is the first step."

Turning on the rented electric sander again Jonathan moved away from the corners and sanded the middle of the room in large continuous sweeps. Rose Ellen, noticing a few places where the machine hadn't reached, started hand-sanding the corners.

"My muscles are beginning to ache," she groaned as she lay facedown on the floor for one weary minute.

"I have just the remedy," Jonathan said gleefully as he bent down and began to massage her back with soft, deliberate movements.

His warm hands sent waves of sensation coursing through her body before common sense triumphed, making her scramble to her feet.

"Hey!" she protested indignantly.

"The working man's vibrator." Jonathan chuckled. He looked at his watch. "It's four o'clock. What do you say we break for the day and get something to eat?"

"All right. But first," she said, waving at the dusty air with a dustier hand, "I think I'd like to shower."

"Mind if I join you?"

"I certainly do! You go first. I'll wait."

Accepting her offer without even a perfunctory show of reluctance, Jonathan made for the bathroom.

"Want to shake these out for me?" Jonathan was holding his pants out for her from around the partially open bathroom door.

There was an unnatural thudding in her heart as she took the proferred pants. Leaning out the window, she watched the pants legs dancing in the breeze and smiled.

Within minutes Jonathan was out, a towel wrapped around his waist. His hair lay wet and glistening on his neck.

"Let me get you another towel." RoseEllen ran to the linen closet and got out one of her new velvety Fieldcrests that her mother had given her on her last visit.

"Thanks. I'll get dressed in here while you shower."

The bathroom was steamy, puddles were on the floor, and the soap was melting in a pool at the bottom of the tub. It struck her as odd that she, fastidious to a fault about some things, like a neat bathroom, didn't mind the mess. As hot water rained down upon her back, she soaped herself with the soft wool sponge and imagined him standing behind her, his soapy body slithering against hers, his hands sliding and exploring. She shook her head under the hot stream and banished the thought. Turning the Water Pik shower head to massage, she let the water pummel her back. Emerging refreshed, she pulled on a pair of black jeans and a lavender silk shirt that billowed and flowed.

"Where do you want to eat?" RoseEllen asked as she

grabbed her macrame shoulder bag. "There's a new little Japanese restaurant that opened down the street and they're supposed to have fabulous sushi. Let me buy you dinner there."

"*You* buy *me* dinner? Listen, women's lib or no I don't think so, hon."

"I mean just as a way of saying thank you for helping me."

"That's not necessary," he said stiffly.

Sensing his annoyance RoseEllen prodded. "There's nothing wrong with a woman paying once in a while. This isn't the nineteenth century, we're both working people, and I do make a lot of money." She bit her tongue. She shouldn't have said that.

"As far as I'm concerned," Jonathan pronounced with finality, "it's moot. I don't feel like sitting in a restaurant. I want to stretch out, relax. Let's stock up at the Italian market and I'll put together a Roman feast for you at my house."

"*You* cook for *me?* Isn't that un-American?" she mocked as she turned the tables on him.

"I'm going to prove to you that I'm not as hopelessly macho as you think."

"And then I'll prove the theory of relativity to you!" she bantered.

"Where Julia Child and Albert Einstein have failed," he retorted fliply, "Robbins and Wood shall succeed."

She knew that she had mentioned relativity in order to distance herself from Jonathan. Things were going too smoothly and she didn't have a place in her life for a junkman.

She looked at him and her heart lurched. He was sweet, kind, mystifying, and threatening all at once.

"Perhaps we can work on that problem after dinner." RoseEllen smiled.

"No, that's when we'll prove that it's love that makes the world go around. Gravity, rotation, and the earth's axis are all myths."

"Hey!" RoseEllen protested good-naturedly. "I almost flunked physics but still I think I'd be on safer ground if we stuck to relativity!"

"I never discuss anything on an empty stomach. Shall we go?"

In a spirit of gaiety and camaraderie she found herself fairly skipping down her stairs behind him.

The Italian market in south Philadelphia covered several square blocks, its streets teeming with shoppers and merchants. Outside stalls which overflowed with produce left little room for the jostling crowd. Although she generally shied away from crowds, RoseEllen was enjoying the carnivallike atmosphere. Stopping at a stall piled high with tomatoes and salad greens, Jonathan, with studied concentration, was carefully picking out the plumpest, reddest tomatoes. His brow was lined and a deep frown was etched in his face. RoseEllen felt like laughing. If he was able to muster such concentration for so mundane a task, imagine the heights he could have reached in the business world had his life taken a different path. He might have been president of the Bendix Corporation today! She tapped him on the shoulder.

"Why don't you pick out a couple of cantaloupes," he suggested. "I'll be through here in a minute."

"Are you sure you trust me to do that?" she kidded.

Because he was still engrossed in the task of picking out green and red peppers, Jonathan didn't respond. RoseEllen moved to the corner where a skinny, swarthy man was hawking melons. She tried to remember what you were supposed to look for when picking out a cantaloupe. Choosing one melon, she shook it, held it to her ear, and smelled it. It smelled like a cantaloupe. The vendor started hollering at her. He grabbed the cantaloupe from her hands.

"No touch, miss. You want, I give you. How many, three, four?"

Taken aback, RoseEllen answered in a small voice, "Two, please." From the bunch nearest him the man picked two large cantaloupes and put them in a paper bag. RoseEllen could just catch a glimpse of the white striated lines on the thick skins before the man was holding out his hand for the money. White lines were good, she thought. That meant the fruit was ripe. Reaching for her wallet she spied Jonathan, who was heading for her.

"What have you got there?" he asked.

She held out the bag for his inspection. Picking up one of the two melons he pressed it with his thumb and index fingers, leaving a large dent.

"What are you giving the lady?" he asked the man as he shoved the bag at him. "She paid you good money, didn't she?" The man nodded. "Then you give her good fruit."

"Okay, mister. Here, you want, you pick."

Even before he had gotten permission, Jonathan was sifting through the pile. "Come here. Let me show you what to look for in a cantaloupe."

"Never mind. You just get what you want," RoseEllen answered, chagrined.

Grinning at her discomfort, Jonathan told her to meet him at the sausage store on the next block. "Ask him for six ounces of prosciutto, the good stuff."

64

"Aye, aye," she answered in a miffed voice.

The sausage store was small, with shelves lining the walls which held imported delicacies like stuffed anchovies, smoked oysters, capers, and cornichons, the small French pickles, and marinated squid. Bins of small, black, wrinkled olives, large, smooth, green ones, pickled eggplant, and artichoke hearts were mouthwatering. Aromatic cheeses and aging meats hung suspended from the ceiling.

"What can I do for you, *bellisima?* Ah, what a sight for sore old Italian eyes!"

Laughing, RoseEllen told him. As the man began slicing, Jonathan entered.

"Let me have a taste of that, friend," he told the roly-poly counterman. Swallowing the prosciutto, he smiled thinly. "You can put that back in the case. Let's have the special, the stuff you keep back there." He pointed behind the counter.

With a respectful nod, the man obliged. "Do you like a taste first, sir?"

"That's all right. No thanks," Jonathan answered with the supreme self-confidence of one who knows how to handle business people of all sorts. Shrinking into herself, RoseEllen slunk out to wait on the sidewalk.

"I knew there was a reason I shopped at the supermarket," she said lightly as Jonathan emerged.

"What you get here doesn't compare with supermarkets, but you have to know what you're doing or act like you do. The shopkeepers save their best for the connoisseurs. They figure the average housewife won't know the difference. It's almost like going into Saks or Neiman Marcus. You buy your cosmetics and the saleslady will put in a perfume sample if you've bought enough. But unless she knows you you get Estée Lauder. She saves her Opium and Bal à Versailles samples for her best customers."

"From perfume to ham." RoseEllen shook her head. "How do you know all this?"

"It's not from reading textbooks." He laughed. "You live long enough, you get around, you wheel and deal a little and you learn."

"I'll bet you've bought your share of Opium and Bal à Versailles too," she taunted.

"Is that jealousy rearing its head?" He smiled. "Trying to find out about my sordid past?"

"Not at all. I was merely curious."

"I bought the Opium for my mother," Jonathan admitted with a straight face.

*I'll bet,* she thought, and wondered why the idea of him buying Opium for someone rankled. She realized suddenly how little she knew about him.

"Have you ever been married?" she ventured.

"Once, a long time ago," he answered shortly. "What about you?"

"No, never." —

"Why not?"

"I never met anyone I wanted to see every day. And I wanted to know I could make it on my own." She waited. "What happened with your marriage?"

"Divorce. It's a blatantly uninteresting story and anyway, in the distant past," he dismissed her question. "Come on. We've got a couple more stops to make."

Together they bought thin-sliced veal in a butcher shop, mushrooms in another outdoor stall, and two ounces of truffles, the wild, piquant mushroomlike fungus that grows in the woods of southern France.

66

"This is more expensive than caviar!" she gasped as Jonathan laid out an exorbitant amount of money for the truffles.

"You know how these are picked, don't you?" Jonathan asked. "They grow underground and can't be cultivated, so pigs are specially trained to sniff them out. Men spend their days tramping through muddy forests with sows on leashes. For that they deserve to be expensive."

"No argument there. What are you making, anyway? I know the appetizer is melon and prosciutto."

"Veal marsala," he pronounced.

"If you'd told me you were a gourmet cook when we first met I might not have made things so difficult," RoseEllen joked expansively.

"There's lots you don't know about me."

Stealing a glance at him, RoseEllen found that he was doing the same to her. And they both began to laugh. People looked at them oddly, these two carefree adults whose mirth spilled over unselfconsciously while the rest of south Philadelphia was engaged in the serious business of getting the most for the least.

Sinking thankfully into the soft leather seats of his white Porsche, RoseEllen was content to let him go for the wine. She closed her eyes. That she felt happy and free and even protected didn't escape her. It was a nice feeling and an unfamiliar one. The men she usually went out with were pleasant enough. Some were downright charmers. None of them ever made laughter bubble up spontaneously from so deep inside her. But she and Jonathan came from such different worlds! She wouldn't fit in with the friends he must have, the rough and tumble, tattoo wearing, pull yourself up by the bootstrap types, and he, veal marsala or not, wouldn't fit in with her sophisticated friends. And no matter if you had the greatest love, you couldn't live in a vacuum. When he returned he was still wearing a big, open smile, while hers had become somewhat guarded.

His apartment on the fourteenth floor of the Philadelphian made RoseEllen gasp. It was mostly black and white and chrome, with slate floors and a sprinkling of modern sculptures that looked to RoseEllen as though they were probably purchased through the auspices of an elite auction house like Parke-Bernet. A wall-length glass window overlooked the boulevard and the art museum and the river.

"Large, modern apartment, river view, one thousand dollars a month," she quipped. "Well, where are the etchings you told me about?"

"Those are in the bedroom." He leered.

Putting her hands on her hips, RoseEllen pretended exasperation.

"I put them there this morning," he continued jokingly. "I was really hoping to get you on those pulleys I have rigged up to the bed!" Moving behind her, he put his hands on her shoulders.

Without turning around she answered dryly, "You never would have made it as a comedian. It's a good thing you're a junkman—although it's hard to imagine you selling junk, even though from the looks of your car and this apartment you must be selling ten tons of it a day."

He laughed. "Do you think I walk up and down streets all day long shouting, 'I sell old clothes, I buy old clothes?' "

"I don't quite know what to believe about you. That's the trouble."

"Believe"—he moved his hand lightly to her cheek— "that I want you more than I should."

She felt a tension fraught with uncertainty building up around them. Stiffening, she glanced at her watch. "Isn't it about time we ate?"

"Ah, yes. The chef is wasting time." He feigned indifference.

The moment was broken. That she saw him retreat into the kitchen with a feeling akin to disappointment was something she knew she didn't want to face.

"Do you need any help?" she called.

"Relax. You can put some music on if you want, or read the magazines stacked on the TV stand."

Too tired to do either, she sank gratefully into the plush velvet of the nearest sofa. Her conscience got the better of her listening to him puttering around the kitchen. She stood in the doorway of the kitchen and gasped. How did he manage to look both graceful and virile while slicing mushrooms? She tore her eyes away from him, knowing they had lingered on him too long. If she were a sculptress she would sculpt his hands. They were powerful, rough yet sensitive, essentially masculine yet exquisitely graceful. His long, tapered fingers looked as though they could tune a car's engine, play a violin, or please a woman with equal finesse. Then she would sculpt his arms, thick with muscles and veins that stood out even when he relaxed. She would do his lower torso if she were especially adept, as a tribute to junkmen and runners. She could just imagine his hard, lean buttocks. They were probably shaped like two perfect half moons. She blinked her eyes rapidly.

"At least let me set the table," she offered lamely.

But he insisted on doing it himself. The table consisted of a thick slab of glass on a base of rough marble. The centerpiece was the Steuben glass Excalibur ringed by lit candles. The lights were dimmed, creating a dazzling effect. Dinner was served on bloodred Mikasa china bordered in gold and was every bit as delicious as he had led her to believe. The prosciutto which lay on top of the cantaloupe was delicately salty and fat-free. The melon was sweet yet firm. With flourishes and gestures befitting a waiter at a three-star restaurant, Jonathan prepared his own Caesar salad. He rubbed garlic in a wooden bowl, broke an egg with one hand, handled a wire wisk with an expertise that reminded RoseEllen of a drum major and his baton. The veal marsala was tender, buttery, and perfectly coupled with a dry Chablis.

"This is fabulous!" she squealed. "I think I'm in awe of you. My culinary skills begin and end with scrambled eggs."

"You make up for it with other skills, I'm sure," he said assuredly.

"Something tells me I'd do best not respond to that," she jested.

"I was talking about your professional skills." He smiled. "Do you practice hypnosis?"

"I have, on occasion. Why do you want to know?"

"I have a bad habit I want to get rid of."

"Exposing yourself on street corners?" She laughed wickedly.

"One glass of Chablis and you're cracking dirty jokes!" he chided good-humoredly. "What I want to do is to stop smoking. I've kicked the habit now at least two dozen times."

"I'll be glad to hypnotize you. That's just the sort of thing hypnosis can help."

"Maybe we can substitute a little of your black magic for that after-dinner cigarette I'm about to light," he suggested thoughtfully.

Even with a full mouth, RoseEllen giggled. Though she normally didn't give professional advice except in her office, never played parlor psychologist with friends or acquaintances, this was an opportunity she could not miss. To hypnotize Jonathan Wood, to run the show even in so limited a circumstance, would give her a feeling of lovely triumph. The quintessential power play! In a split second's moment of amused lucidity she rued her self-perception. Why did she have to examine her reactions to everything and understand herself so darn well? Her desire to dominate was not a terribly attractive trait.

"Although," Jonathan continued, "I don't know if I can trust you to hypnotize me. What if you have me marching straight to the Russian consulate to defect?"

"Don't worry about that, but I might have you marching up Broad Street in your birthday suit!" she quipped.

"If you're marching with me I won't mind. You're one of the few women I know who probably looks better undressed than dressed, and you don't look bad dressed!"

RoseEllen was glad when, at that moment, he rose to fetch a bowl of Malaga grapes and fresh figs.

"Mmm," she sighed as she bit into a succulently sweet fig. "Do you eat like this often?"

"Only when I'm trying to seduce a young lady." He grinned.

"You only failed by a little bit," she retorted with mock solicitousness. "To get back to hypnosis, I thought you didn't trust psychology. And I believe that when we first met you referred to me as a"—she cleared her throat—"shrink."

"Everything has a purpose," he responded tongue-in-cheek, "even the Med fruit fly!"

"Stop there!" she laughed, knowing full well that he was

teasing. She was learning, she thought, that she should only take about half of what he said seriously. "And now, to allay your fears," she said seriously, "nobody can make a subject do anything under hypnosis which he wouldn't normally do."

Jonathan laughed boldly. "Okay, I'm game. When do we start?"

"You'll really let me hypnotize you?"

"Sure. What do I do? Should I stand up? Do I close my eyes?"

"No, no. Why don't you sit down on the couch?" she suggested. "There. Sit back. Make yourself comfortable. That's fine." Unclasping the gold-and-malachite pendant she had luckily worn around her neck, she tried to quiet her racing heart. "Watch this pendant. Do not take your eyes from it." Almost indiscernibly she moved her fingers, setting the round disk in motion, first slowly to and fro and then faster and faster. "Relax. Empty your mind of all thought." Her voice was soothing. "R-e-l-a-x. R-e-l-a-x. Your toes are beginning to feel loose. The tension is draining out of your toes. Now concentrate on your feet. Your feet feel unconfined as if they're dangling in a cool stream. R-e-l-a-x. Think about your calves. The muscles feel supple and tingly as if they've just been massaged. All the tension, all the stress is pouring out of your calves. Out! Out! Your thighs are rubbery and limp and sooooo relaxed"—*and* what *thighs!* she thought as she stifled the giggle which welled up in her throat. "The tautness is pouring out of your body now, your hips, your stomach, your chest, think about each part of your body and how good it feels. Let your chest sag. Take deep breaths to cleanse your lungs. That's good. You feel clean and relax-

72

ed. Let your shoulders go, your neck. Concentrate on your neck. All the tension is going to one spot.

"Now"—she steeled herself for her next words which she knew to be an essential part of the hypnotic process— "I'm going to rub your neck. Each time you feel my hands on you think of all the tension that's pouring out of your body and into my hands. I'm going to take it all. Let your head hang forward on your chest. It wants to hang down. You couldn't hold it up if you tried." She watched his head drop onto his chest as she moved behind him. Her hand trembled as she let it lie on his nape. In small, circular motions she massaged deeply yet gently. His skin felt like raw silk covering the column of solid muscle; his hair, dark and thick, felt like the spun, finished product. Though she had practiced the art of hypnotic massage a few times before, she had never executed it with such intimacy.

She thought she heard a low sound, almost like a groan of satisfaction. No, it must have been her imagination. Jonathan was sitting perfectly still, his eyes closed. He was clearly in the first stage of a hypnotic trance. "There is nothing in your mind, nothing exists. There is only my hand on your neck and the deep restfulness you feel. Your eyes are shut tightly now. You cannot open them for they are stuck together. Try to open them. You will see that you cannot."

Moving in front of him she observed his eyelids flutter but remain closed. She assumed a look of immense satisfaction as she returned to the back of his chair and to the neck massage. As her white fingers kneaded his darker flesh the image of herself as conqueror flashed before her mind and she flushed at the nonsensical thought. "You are asleep. It is a deep sleep, a restful, full sleep, and when you awake you will feel refreshed and energetic. We are going to talk about cigarettes. Everything that goes on here will be clearly and accurately remembered when you awake. You will awaken when I snap my fingers, not before."

She stood in front of him again. Good Lord, was he handsome! Her eyes followed a path from his head down to his toes, the same path that his eyes had blazed when he first saw her. Her eyes lingered at his chest and for a brief moment her hands itched to run through his chest hair. She wondered how he would like being ogled by a woman. No more than most women did, she guessed. Her eyes lit briefly on his face. He was deep in a hypnotic trance. Forcing herself to get on with it, she slipped her malachite pendant around her neck.

"From the time you awaken you will feel no desire for cigarettes. You will enjoy the feeling of cleanliness in your lungs. Instead of reaching for a cigarette you will take deep breaths of fresh air. As more and more time elapses from the time you last smoked you will experience an increasing sensation of well-being. Your mind is empty now except for my words. You will not smoke again. Your craving for cigarettes will diminish with each passing day until you are left with no desire at all to smoke. You will be filled with a sense of pride and accomplishment at giving up cigarettes and you will feel better than you ever felt before. You are still relaxed. Your mind is clear. When you awaken you will remember my words. I shall snap my fingers now and you will wake up, rested but energetic."

RoseEllen knew she was smiling a Cheshire smile as she looked at the man seated before her. With a flourish she snapped the fingers of both hands in unison. A surge of power coursed through her: with her brandishments his eyes would slowly open . . . except that they didn't. She snapped again, louder this time. "You will awaken. Wake up!" For the third time she snapped. For the fourth. Her fingers were smarting. "When I snap my fingers once more, your eyes will open. You will be wide awake!" Her voice was edgy. Swinging her arms from the shoulders, putting her whole body into it, with a great big breath, she snapped. She felt the wind created by the sweeping of her arms. His face was implacable, calm, relaxed—and still asleep.

RoseEllen paced his living room, her panic mounting, and glancing down saw that she was wringing her hands, something she had never done before. What a fool she was! She should never have hypnotized him. Her experience with hypnosis had been far too limited to have risked it in a social situation with someone she barely knew. What if he never came out of it? She felt herself on the verge of hysteria. What if he became a vegetable? Forcing herself to calm down she tried to remember all that she had ever read about hypnotherapy. She sat down next to Jonathan, closed her eyes, and thought hard. In her mind's eye she could picture the place on the page of her clinical psychology book which dealt with waking the subject. It was in the lower right column of the left hand page. She squeezed her eyes tighter. It was coming to her now! The book had said that it was almost impossible for a subject not to wake up at the proper cue. Such a deep state of hypnosis was rarely reached and then only in special circumstances. A subject would have to be hypnotized many times in succession and would, each time, have to reach a deeper state in the hypnotic trance. Failure to respond to a hypnotist's signal was usually due to chicanery. Anger

75

replaced her anxiety. Fuming, she rose. So! He was tricking her, playing a little game! Had she not been so unnerved by him she might have realized it sooner. Well, two could play! Tiptoeing in front of him, she thought she saw him composing his features. His timing, she thought angrily, was off by a second.

"In addition to giving up cigarettes, Jonathan, you will give up sex! Instead, you will take up Zen and meditation!"

"All right! All right!" He laughed hoarsely as his eyes flew open. "Had you going there for a little bit, didn't I?"

"You're awake. How nice!" She flashed him a saccharine smile. "I hope you enjoyed yourself."

"Thanks. I did."

RoseEllen shot him an utterly exasperated look. Her anger had not abated. "Why are you trying to make my life difficult?"

"I'm not," he protested with a hurt expression on his face. "It wasn't my fault that I turned out to be a poor subject for hypnosis. So I decided to have a little fun. Aren't you having fun?"

"Terrific fun," she said drolly. "So much fun that I think I'd better leave before I die laughing."

"Don't go."

Arching a dubious eyebrow, RoseEllen responded in her coolest voice. "Thanks for helping me today and for dinner. Oh, and don't worry about driving me home. I'll take the bus."

"Go if you want, but there's no way I'm going to let you take a bus alone at night," Jonathan thundered.

Indignation blazed in her eyes. "May I remind you that this is 1983. Women have the vote and they're allowed in buses, front as well as back. It's barely eight thirty. I can take care of myself and if you try and stop me I'll deck you!"

Jonathan burst out laughing. "I do believe you said all that in one breath. Feisty, feisty. It's quite charming." He leaned negligently against a bookcase. "So you'll deck me? You'll need some extra fortification for that. How about a snifter of cognac?"

She met his laughter with a poise she didn't feel. "All right. But just pour me a touch."

He poured the Rémy Martin into a heavy crystal snifter. Not a drinker, and remembering belatedly that one was supposed to sniff and savor cognac, she took a big gulp which burned all the way down her throat to her stomach.

"That hit the spot." She grimaced despite herself. "Listen, if it will make you happy I'll take a cab home."

"What will make me happy is if you stay. The cab will simply allay my fears."

"And your male chauvinism," she added snippily.

"I'm not so bad, am I?" he asked winningly.

She paused before answering. "I guess not. Actually, you're kind of nice." She swallowed hard. "Good night."

At the door she turned around. "Weren't you hypnotized at all? Even a little?"

"I told you I'm a bad subject. No one would ever be able to hypnotize me," he said matter-of-factly.

"So why did you let me make a fool of myself?"

"You weren't making a fool of yourself. You were cute."

"Little girls and puppy dogs are cute, Jonathan," she retorted cuttingly. "I'm a grown woman."

The last thing she saw before closing the door was the amused twinkle in his eye and the utterly phony expres-

77

sion of contriteness which he had assumed.

RoseEllen swept through the lobby of the Philadelphi-an, for the second time barely noticing its elegance. The doorman blew his whistle, conjuring up a taxi for her as if by magic.

As the taxi sped toward Society Hill RoseEllen's spirits plummeted. She should be angry at Jonathan for his cha-rade. Instead, she found the whole episode amusing, though she would never admit that to him. With her flailing arms snapping furiously and the desperation which must have shown in her face, it surely would have made a superb *Candid Camera* segment. She shivered. Rolling up the rear windows she thought that it had been a lovely day and wondered why she was speeding toward her topsy-turvy apartment when she could be with Jona-than. Because, she told herself firmly, it wouldn't do to get involved with a man like that. They were too different, inside and out. But it had been a long time since she had wanted a man, and she *did* want him. She wanted to feel his arms around her and she wanted his kisses. She wanted all of him. No! she told herself. It was wrong! Casual sex was wrong. It left you feeling empty and used. And what more could it be with him? There was no future in it but there could be pain. She was a therapist and the last person in the world to self-destruct. Hadn't she always been judi-cious? Never the one to push herself beyond endurance, whether in a high-school dance marathon, a college M&M's eating contest, or in the relationships she had had that were more trouble than they were worth. Why, at the ripe old age of twenty-eight, should she start mak-ing mistakes? Faltering, she leaned toward the driver. How thrilling, how daring, how unlike her it would be for her to tell him to turn around and take her back to the Philadelphian. She leaned back in the cool, cracked seat again—and kept her silence.

She wasn't altogether surprised when Jonathan appeared at her door bright and early the next day, Sunday.

"I never leave a job half finished," he explained to her.

They spent most of the day sanding and painting. Jonathan applied the polyurethane on the floor and did a good deal of the painting. What remained for RoseEllen to finish in the living room would easily be accomplished in a day. The rest of the day was passed in a spirit of easy, happy companionship. There was no pressure, none of the innuendos which made her nervous; there was astonishingly little reserve on her part. The only disappointment was when he couldn't stay for dinner. It wouldn't have been much of a dinner compared to his, she told him modestly. She had been intending to broil a couple of steaks, throw together a salad, and open a can of beans. His sincerity was genuine when he told her how sorry he was, but his earlier plans were unbreakable and, believe it or not, with an elderly aunt.

On Monday RoseEllen put on the finishing touches of paint, buffed the floors with a machine she had rented from the hardware store, and pushed the furniture back in place. When she opened the door to the noontime knock she knew in advance who it would be. And there he stood, with a great big rubber plant in his arms and a bagful of Philadelphia cheese steaks getting squashed between his elbow and ribs. Because he had to get back to work it was a short visit. He was going out of town that night for two days and had some loose ends to tie up before he left.

"What in the world could be so urgent about the junk

business?" she teased. "Has there been a plane crash somewhere, a train derailment?"

He laughed at her and promised to call. He did—four times on Tuesday and five on Wednesday. Every time the phone rang RoseEllen found herself grinning ear to ear.

# CHAPTER FIVE

As she opened the morning mail RoseEllen had the same self-satisfied expression that she had been wearing of late. There was a letter from Aruna, her foster child in Calcutta, reminding her that her sixth birthday was a mere two weeks off. RoseEllen smiled fondly, glad that she had a birthday present, a lovely hand-smocked dress, wrapped and ready to be mailed. Even though the agency formally disapproved of extra gifts, RoseEllen made sure to send each of her "adopted" children a birthday present.

Noting that there was nothing else of interest in the mail, she sat down to read the newspaper. She scanned the front page, not really seeing what was written there, for in her mind's eye Jonathan's face faded in and out of focus. Absentmindedly she sipped a half cup of lukewarm coffee that was sitting on the table. As she turned the pages an ad for a special preseason opera caught her eye. In order to benefit the arts, the great tenor Placido Domingo was going to be singing the part of Don Jose in *Carmen,* with Anna Moffo singing the female lead. An avid opera buff since the age of eighteen, RoseEllen felt her pulse quicken. This was something she could not miss. She ran to find her credit card, dialed Ticketron, and thanked her stars for having got two of the last seats still available. When she hung up she forgot about the French toast she was going to make for breakfast and instead started straightening up the apartment. Just as she was watering her new rubber plant the phone rang. She hoped it was Jonathan. He was coming back late that afternoon from the trip he had had to extend and she could hardly wait to tell him about the tickets.

"I hate opera," he said flatly.

"What?"

"I'm dying to see you, RoseEllen, but there's no way you're getting me to that opera. I hate opera."

"How can you say that? Opera is one of the highest art forms. It's beautiful!"

"To each his own. If you like it so much, go. But without me. And I promise not to lure you to a boxing match with me!"

"You like boxing? And you hate opera?" Her voice wilted. "How could you?"

"I'm just being honest, babe," he said in his cavalier way. "And I'll bet that half of your audience tonight would rather be at a boxing match or in front of the television. They go because opera is high culture and they ought to support it—and be seen supporting it. During intermission they all prance and preen about in their Nipons and Pierre Cardins. No thanks."

"Not the people I know. They go to the opera for the opera."

"Hmm. I know the type." He was clearly unimpressed. "And afterward they go to the Terrace *for* the Terrace." He sarcastically named one of Philadelphia's chic après-theater spots.

"How did you get so cynical?"

"Don't you mean uncouth?" he teased. "Well, my lady shrink, I picked it up on the street. You learn what it's all about on the street. After the opera why not take a cab over here? I missed you."

"No thanks. I'll probably be at the Terrace too late to do anything else," she retorted spitefully.

"Toss out a couple of bravos for me, will you?"

The phone went dead in her hands and RoseEllen thought that one more exasperating trait that Jonathan Wood had was his habit of ending phone conversations without a proper good-bye.

Flopping on her sofa she thought that she wouldn't go to the opera either. It was spoiled for her now. Since she couldn't very well throw away sixty dollars she would give the tickets to the Rileys. And she did owe Dr. Riley. At least three of her clients were his referrals. Half-heartedly she leafed through her address book for his home number.

"What a lovely gesture!" Mrs. Riley cooed when RoseEllen had made known the purpose of her call. "We do adore the opera! I suppose you didn't know about my toe though. I broke it recently so here I sit with a pound of plaster on my foot. I have a *splendid* idea! Why don't you go with Dr. Riley? He would be so pleased and I do feel awfully guilty making him sit here at home with me all the time."

"Um, I, uh," RoseEllen stammered.

"Oh, he'll be delighted." Mrs. Riley laughed gaily. "We're probably going to miss most of the season when it comes and all the parties and things. What time does it start? About eight? Why don't you meet him right outside the Academy then? It is at the Academy, of course?" Mrs. Riley went on and on, asking one question after another without waiting for an answer. "Placido Domingo is my favorite tenor. Such a handsome man, especially after he lost all that weight. Did you see him on the Carson show? He was marvelous, just marvelous. He sang 'I Left My Heart in San Francisco' and he simply sent shivers up and down my spine."

"Actually, Mrs. Riley, isn't there someone else . . . ?"

"Oh dear! There's the doorbell," Mrs. Riley cut in. "Such a bother to have to answer with this foot. I'll tell the doctor about your invitation. So thoughtful of you."

For the second time in the space of a few minutes, RoseEllen, with mounting irritation, was left holding a dead phone. There was nothing to be done now. She couldn't risk insulting the Rileys by reneging so she might as well make the best of it. She lay down on her bed. Why hadn't she followed her instincts? When she had first spoken with Jonathan she knew he wasn't her type. It was always a mistake to force something that wasn't meant to be. Well, thank her lucky stars that she hadn't gone back to his apartment the other night. Even so, it was too late for her to regret her involvement with him. It was undeniable that she couldn't go half an hour without thinking about him, without remembering something he had said or the special way he had looked when he touched her. What in the world was going to happen? They had so little in common. What they shared was little more than a passing dalliance, for you couldn't build a relationship on wit and jokes. When the jokes dried up they would have nothing left. But why was she even thinking like that, as if there were ever the possibility that this could be a long-term thing?

Anyway, if he really did care about her he would have made an effort to enjoy the opera. He would have tried it, just to please her. He was simply too set in his ways. It was important to have an idea of who you were, but Jonathan, it seemed (despite his devil-may-care veneer), was as rigid as the scrap metal he bought and sold. And she would be darned before she would give up the things she enjoyed—

opera, ballet, theater, even poetry. Jonathan's idea of fun was a splash in a public fountain and a good fight. Well, she would never trade Placido Domingo for Sugar Ray Robinson! On the other hand, it had been kind of fun wading in that fountain. She wouldn't, of course, want to make a habit of such wild behavior. Imagine if some roving photographer had caught a shot of them and put it in the People section of *The Philadelphia Inquirer.* That would have cost her a referral or two, and maybe even a client.

RoseEllen wished she could stop thinking. She had never before felt so fiery an attraction to a man and yet refused him, had never before become obsessed and driven by a man. She had to fight with herself to keep from calling him and telling him that she wouldn't go to the opera because, more than anything, she wanted to be with him. Why was this happening to her? Why now? And why this man? He was a man who would probably spend his spare time stupefied before a television set when she wanted to listen to Mozart or talk. They were worlds apart. He was pushy and too aggressive. He didn't play by the rules. That was fine when you were a kid but not now. The stakes were too high. This was her life and she wasn't going to throw it away.

*This is my husband, the junkman,* she thought. *How would that sound?* But how disgusting she was, she berated herself. Could this really be RoseEllen Robbins who was thinking the thoughts of an intellectual snob? She wasn't like that, not really. It was just, she rationalized, that she had worked so hard to get where she was. It hadn't come easily to her. She didn't come from money. She had waitressed her way through college and graduate school. And she still had debts to finish paying. All her life she had wanted to make something of herself. And she was succeeding, doing it on her own, with no help from anybody. She didn't want to end up old and unaccomplished, thinking that she could have done this and she could have done that. She had seen that happen to her own mother, a wonderfully bright woman with an utterly broken spirit who spent her days trying to stretch her husband's meager income.

But Jonathan was clearly well to do, she thought. Even with her income she could not afford his apartment. But more important than his net worth, she grimaced to herself, was the way he thought. Jonathan disliked psychology. To dislike a person's chosen field of endeavor would be to dislike that person, she reasoned. You couldn't separate the two. And then, he disliked opera. So her vocation and her avocations would be taboo. What would they talk about? He would soon tire of spending all his time trying to get her into bed!

Jumping up, RoseEllen paced back and forth in her freshly painted living room. She reminded herself of a caged animal—brimming with energy and anger and desperately unhappy. Why, oh why hadn't he said he would come with her? Then, at least, her castle in the air would have stayed aloft awhile longer.

With an energy born of frustration RoseEllen spent the remainder of the afternoon emptying out every drawer in the house and throwing out clothes that were old or irreparably soiled or unflattering, and even some that were not.

When it came time to dress for the opera, RoseEllen reached for her black jersey Halston. She stopped her hand in mid-air, remembering Jonathan's Cardin–Nipon remark about operagoers' evening wear. Instead she chose a simple suit that she had owned, she thought, for at least a hundred years.

Dr. Riley was waiting on the sidewalk for her in front of the Academy of Music. As she approached RoseEllen blinked twice. He was dressed to the nines in a tuxedo.

"Good evening, Rosey," he boomed over the melee created by vocal operagoers with their "Hello, darlings."

"Hi, Dr. Riley. I hope you haven't been waiting long," RoseEllen said as she hurried to meet him.

"No, no. I've enjoyed it. I met some people I know."

They entered the Academy and took their seats. When the orchestra began to play the overture to *Carmen* RoseEllen felt her spirits lift. The music was gay, exhilarating, and courageous. She became mesmerized as the production swung into the first act. The sweet, liquid tones of Placido's voice carried her far away to the sunny Mediterranean. It was a magical voice, erotic, velvety, and deep, a Stradivarius among voices. When she heard the familiar "Flower Song" and "Toreador Song" she could barely restrain herself from applauding. The hall was hushed, the silence rarely broken by even a cough. The only distraction for RoseEllen was from the incessant rustling of paper as Dr. Riley leafed through the program. But even that didn't do much to disturb her, for besides the great music the story of the gypsy girl, Carmen—a story of passion, unrequited love, jealousy, and death—was believable and in itself good theater. There were times when RoseEllen found herself so moved by the music that she yearned to grab someone's arm, preferably Jonathan's. Since the only arms available happened to belong to a stranger on one side and to Dr. Riley on the other, she squeezed her own arm.

At the first intermission RoseEllen was still under the music's spell as she accompanied her escort to the lobby.

"What incredible artists they are!" she breathed.

"Incredible" Dr. Riley seconded.

"Miss Robbins! Dr. Riley!" Wilson Beck, her secretary, swaggered over to them with a pretty young blonde in tow. "You didn't tell me last week that you were coming here," he said reproachfully.

"I didn't know last week," RoseEllen answered coolly.

"How's your vacation? I'll bet you can't wait to get back to work." He smiled ingratiatingly.

RoseEllen smiled noncommittally.

"How do you like the performance?" she asked.

"It's grand," he answered quickly.

"Just divine." His date nodded solemnly.

RoseEllen noticed Dr. Riley restlessly scanning the crowd. The universally accepted timetable of one minute per acquaintance per intermission (with a ten-minute intermission and luck you could greet six couples) had been surpassed. It was time to move on.

It seemed that all of Philadelphia's "high society" was here. RoseEllen wondered briefly how she had missed the announcement of this event until this morning. With Dr. Riley's deft maneuvering they managed to wave or speak to, RoseEllen thought wryly, at least half of the city's untitled nobility. She was getting the uncomfortable feeling that, for most of the attendees, this was more of a social event than a musical event. Maybe Jonathan had been right about that. If it hadn't been for Jonathan, she wondered, would she have had so jaundiced a view of the chitchat she heard? She wondered if she would have noticed how many of the women managed to wave their hands tirelessly in the air, punctuating each one of their comments with a gesture that caused brilliant flashes of jeweled light to bounce off the walls?

During the second intermission custom was flouted and RoseEllen found herself listening to Dr. Riley expound for almost eight minutes on a business deal with an elderly gentleman who was introduced to RoseEllen as a retired psychoanalyst.

"I got involved with this condominium conversion deal through a young fellow—Jonathan Wood's the name," Dr. Riley said to the man.

RoseEllen's ears perked up.

"The man usually knows what he's talking about. He's made a lot of money and I let him talk me into this one." Dr. Riley turned to RoseEllen. "Why Rosey, you know who I'm talking about. The young fellow you were dancing with at our party!"

"Oh!" RoseEllen said, startled. "Yes, um, that *was* Jonathan Wood."

"Anyway, as I was saying, he really railroaded me into this one. I suppose I shouldn't blame him. He couldn't know what a headache this would turn out to be."

"What happened with it?" the older man asked.

Dr. Riley hit his head with his fist. "Tenant unions, rent strikes, bad press. . . . You name it, we've had it. Better to stick with stocks and bonds."

"You said it," the other man agreed. "Why would you want to get involved with that anyway?"

*Greed,* RoseEllen thought, though she didn't like the thought.

"It will turn out right for us," Dr. Riley continued, "but it's a messy business and an expensive one."

Shocked, RoseEllen was glad when the bell rang signaling the end of the intermission and the start of the third act.

The tragic, gripping, passionate finale was ruined for her. All she could think about was Jonathan and Dr. Riley in cahoots to throw people out of their apartments so they could reap enormous profits. Though she hadn't heard all the details she could imagine the scenario and all her sympathies were with the tenants. Junk was one thing. Inhumanity was another. You certainly could never tell about people. Here was Dr. Riley, widely touted as the compassionate founder of a new outpatient clinic that would treat underprivileged children for free in addition to the regular therapy it offered to its more prosperous clients. That was good publicity, Rose Ellen thought angrily. There weren't many poor children who would make use of that offer. Those children would only receive help when their problems were so severe as to require they be institutionalized. So Dr. Riley's clinic would be useless to them. But that was Dr. Riley, and what he did was no concern of hers.

Jonathan. She had almost been ready to forgive him his philistine ways. And now she had to learn that not only did he scorn psychology, not only was he totally uninterested in opera, but he was the worst kind of hustler, the kind with little regard for the human suffering he caused. She almost felt like picking up a placard and marching with those tenants. Maybe she would.

When the last curtain fell, the audience jumped to its feet to applaud. Dr. Riley shouted with the rest. RoseEllen clapped till her hands smarted.

"Let's go to the Terrace for a little bite," Dr. Riley whispered conspiratorially.

90

RoseEllen blanched. This couldn't be happening! It was as if Jonathan had written the script.

"I can't. I'm on a diet," she lied. "I'll bet if you try you can find someone else to go with, though. You seem to know enough people." She hoped she had kept the biting edge out of her voice. What Dr. Riley did was of no concern to her except where their professional interests happened to coincide.

"Now, Rosey," he admonished, "no one goes right home after the opera. Mrs. Riley isn't expecting me."

Dr. Mitchell Lewis and his wife approached. "You all going to the Terrace?" he drawled winningly. "We'll see you there. RoseEllen, I want to tell you about a seminar I attended last week at the University of Pennsylvania. It's on humor therapy. Perhaps you can use a tidbit or two in that talk you're giving. It's on paradox therapy, isn't it?"

RoseEllen nodded eagerly. Dr. Lewis was one of Dr. Riley's staff clinicians and a very bright man. She looked forward to hearing what he had to say.

"Well, maybe."

"So," Dr. Riley said with a jocular smile, "she won't go to the Terrace if I ask her but agrees when you do. I'd watch out if I were you, Bette," he kidded Dr. Lewis's wife.

"Dr. Riley," RoseEllen addressed him with a miffed expression on her face, "the problem with hanging around with a bunch of therapists is that everything you say and do is analyzed to death. It's interesting, I'll admit, but can lead to some very inaccurate conclusions."

"Do you mean to say"—Bette Lewis laughed throatily —"that you're not waiting with bated breath to seduce my treasure of a husband?"

"Sorry." RoseEllen laughed in an equally sophisticated

way. "I'm already spoken for." She stopped short, not having intended to say that. She didn't even know if it were true.

"Who's the mystery man?" Bette asked coyly.

"No one you know."

"She's holding out on us," Dr. Lewis joined in. "Quick, somebody get the truth serum! I just hope he's not another psychologist. That would never work."

Not used to having her personal life the object of scrutiny, at least in her presence, RoseEllen blushed furiously. "He's far from it."

The Terrace was crowded with the after-theater crowd. There was much table hopping and exclamations of joy as those people who had been seated in the left mezzanine at the opera greeted those whom they had missed because they were seated on the orchestra right. RoseEllen was getting dizzy with all the air-kissing. She had learned a long time ago that when you wore lipstick you only kissed the air next to people's cheeks. The evening stretched into the early morning hours and RoseEllen found herself alternately interested and bored by the conversations, especially when all anybody had to say about Placido Domingo was how much money he made or to tell the latest episode of his much-publicized feud with the other leading tenor, Luciano Pavarotti.

She picked at her quiche and found herself wondering what Jonathan was doing. One thing was for sure. He would never be sitting here where the air-conditioning was on the blink, scrunched up at a small table listening to hoity-toity opera gossip. In this heat, she thought amusedly, he would probably be out looking for the nearest fountain!

Whatever was happening to her? It used to be that when

she went out with colleagues she was totally involved in the conversation. Now she was sitting back and looking at it critically. Now she was picking at her quiche and sipping her white wine and wishing it were a hot dog and Coke. Maybe she was becoming unhinged. Anybody in her right mind knew that quiche was better! And anybody in her right mind would hang on to every witty, urbane, and elegant word that was uttered here. She tried to envision Drs. Riley and Lewis or any of the others in her apartment on their hands and knees helping her with her floors. She couldn't. She tried to imagine herself making love to any of the men here. That was even worse. She imagined it in exquisite detail with Jonathan. Could she be falling in love? The thought struck her with the force of a thunderbolt. She didn't want it to be true. Yet she kept coming back to it. Jonathan Wood not only intrigued her. He held her captive. He might not be as well versed in the same subjects as her colleagues, but he made them appear shallow. When he said something you knew he meant it. And when he talked trivia he didn't pretend it was something deeper. But he was a scoundrel! He was ruthless in business and in his personal life. He had hunted her as a predator hunts his prey. And he would discard her when he was through with her. He had made no promises. She should have no illusions. Men like Jonathan Wood and women like RoseEllen Robbins didn't get serious. With her professional status and prudish ways she was a challenge to him. And why should she want someone like him? Better a surgeon or a CPA. But why was her mind so muddied and everything so complicated?

"A penny for your thoughts." Dr. Riley poked her in the ribs.

"I bet I know what she's thinking about." Bette Lewis smirked.

"Piaget and his Stages of Development." RoseEllen twinkled.

"Piaget never made anyone's eyes glaze over like yours," Bette retorted. "I'll bet you wish you were somewhere else—or at least *with* someone else."

"I'm having a good time," RoseEllen protested.

"I'm going to walk you out. I have a feeling that you have places to go where none of us can follow," Bette commented dryly.

Attention at the table was riveted on Bette and RoseEllen.

"Get your shawl," Bette ordered firmly.

Acquiescing, RoseEllen said her good-byes. Dr. Riley, when he stood to thank her again for the ticket, mumbled apologetically that he hoped he hadn't taken her away from something else that she preferred doing.

"No, no. It was a nice evening." RoseEllen smiled. "I'm glad you came."

Fearing that Bette would pump her for information on the way out, RoseEllen told her to stay put.

"Take it easy," Bette advised. "If it causes you anguish it might not be worth it."

That night, RoseEllen lay in bed, her eyes wide open watching the pattern of car headlights on her ceiling. Bette's words stuck with her. Jonathan *did* cause her anguish. Worse than that she was causing herself. On the one hand, she had felt critical of her friends. On the other, she felt guilty. They were basically good people. Nobody was perfect and she had never before expected perfection from her friends or colleagues. And she had never before looked at an audience critically. Whether or not they appreciated

94

what was happening on the stage wasn't her business. She came to the painful conclusion that she didn't like herself too much right now. And she didn't like the influence that was shaping her thoughts. Better to cut it off now before something happened that would make it too devastating. Jonathan and she were too different. And she, more than anybody, should be responsible for her actions. She could not be responsible for a chemical attraction, but she could choose her course of action. At last she fell into a fitful sleep.

# CHAPTER SIX

How should she introduce the talk? She had always heard that the opening was the most important part of a talk because it's there that a speaker hooks or loses an audience. The meeting was tomorrow night. That gave her two days to write and practice the presentation. It would be a milestone in her career, showing her to be not only a competent practitioner but also a fine theoretician. Paradox therapy was a controversial form of therapy and if not done correctly could do immeasurable harm to the patient.

She flicked the switch of her electric typewriter on and off. Should she start with a joke or an anecdote? They said that was an effective way to put the audience at ease. But this was a group of therapists. They would be wise to any such facile techniques. But they, too, were human. All right, she finally decided. She would start with an anecdote. But which one?

She accidentally hit some keys on the typewriter. Pulling her paper out she crumpled it up, threw it on the floor, and inserted a fresh sheet. She rose to make herself a cup of tea. Carrying it back to her bedroom where she had set up the typewriter, she spilled a few drops on the floor and bent to wipe it up with a napkin. She typed *page 1* on the paper. Except that she pressed the *i* instead of the *1*. New sheet. She brought the cup to her lips. The tea was too bitter. She went back into the kitchen for more water. Where were those shortbread biscuits she had bought the other day? Searching in her haphazardly arranged cabinets she found the biscuits on the spice shelf. She might as well eat them in the dining room with her tea, she decided.

She glanced at the wall telephone. What was he doing now, anyway? Why didn't he call? Maybe she could just dial his number to see if he were home and then hang up when he answered. *How childish!* she berated herself. She'd better get back to work. Get back to it! She laughed wryly. She hadn't even started it! At this rate she would stand up in front of the association to do a soft shoe!

She swallowed her cookie, picked up her teacup, and seated herself once again at the typewriter. This time she did a little better. *What is a paradox?* she started. *Goldberg and Rubin—a pair o' docs up in the Bronx.* Hah, hah, she thought disgustedly, not sure at all whether her corny attempt at a definition would go over with the oh-so-serious therapists who made up the association. She ripped the paper out of the typewriter, crumpling up yet another sheet. The floor, strewn with paper balls, was at least giving her the illusion that she was working, she mused. She drew a deep breath. Jonathan Wood had the most wonderful body. Stop it! She ought to give herself ten lashes, she thought. How could a sophisticated, hard-working woman like herself be reduced to sniveling, adolescent behavior? This was simply additional proof that Jonathan was not for her. A man, if he meant anything, should enhance one's feelings about oneself, not destroy them. RoseEllen was competent, cool, controlled. This lovestruck woman whose skin she had temporarily assumed was no one she recognized.

The phone rang. The teacup full of smoky-flavored Lapsang Souchoung toppled off the typing table as RoseEllen made a dash for the receiver. Looking back at the pool of amber liquid on her newly stripped and waxed floor, she hoped it wouldn't have time to sink in before she could wipe it up.

"Hello."

"Hi."

"Could you hold on for a second, Jonathan?" She ran to the kitchen, picked up a roll of paper towels, unrolled several sheets, and not even taking the time to tear them off from the roll, dropped the whole thing on the puddle.

"Hello, again." Her voice was breathless.

"How was your night at the opera?"

"Great. How was your evening?"

"Terrible. I should have been with you," he admitted.

"You could have been," she replied pointedly.

"Why don't you come over here and we'll make up for lost time. I have a nice, soft bed you haven't tried yet."

RoseEllen had a queasy feeling in her stomach. He *was* only interested in one thing. "I have work to do."

"Do it later."

"It won't wait," she said firmly.

"Then I'll come over there and help. Didn't I prove to you once already what a good worker I am?"

"I'm afraid you couldn't help with this." She laughed haughtily, wanting to hurt him as he had just hurt her. "It's quite esoteric."

"What are you doing," he kidded, "retranslating the Rosetta stone?"

"I'm preparing a talk for a professional meeting."

"Oh yes? Where? I'll be in the front row with a bouquet of roses when you take your final bows."

"No thanks. I don't think I want you within a mile of the place. It's an important talk and actually I wouldn't put it past you to do something like that." She couldn't keep the hint of laughter from her voice. A bouquet of roses, indeed!

"How about if I pick you up for dinner then?"

"Dinner? Dinner?" she repeated blankly.

"Yes. You know, where two people order food with French-sounding names, sip the proper wine, and engage in witty repartee."

"I can't. I'll just have time to throw together a sandwich for dinner."

"Isn't this your vacation?" Jonathan pursued relentlessly. "Why are you working?"

"I don't know." She shrugged even though he couldn't see. "I guess it's important to me. There are certain fields of human endeavor," she said arrogantly, "that you don't want to stop thinking about, that you're committed to." She would show him, she thought. She might just be a potentially warm body to him but to the rest of the people who knew her she was a lot more. "What are you committed to—besides junk and the perfect prosciutto?"

Jonathan didn't answer right away. RoseEllen thought frantically that she had gone too far. But isn't that what she wanted? End it now. It was for the best.

"What are you doing tomorrow?" he asked after a long pause.

"More of the same."

"All work and no play . . ."

"Make a very successful girl," she finished.

"A very unpredictable girl," he corrected her. "You remind me a bit of those cannibalistic flowers that eat whatever unsuspecting thing flies too close."

"At least I don't remind you of a scorpion. They eat their mates!"

99

"I doubt if you'd ever get that opportunity." His voice was chilling.

They said barely cordial good-byes. RoseEllen felt as if she had just mugged somebody and at the same time as if she had just been mugged, and as if it had been her own fault for walking through a dark, deserted alley in a bad part of town at midnight.

She picked up the soggy roll of paper towels, ascertained that the floor had not been damaged by the tea, and forced herself to spend the remainder of the day at her typewriter. Now that that was over, she rationalized, there was nothing to keep her from concentrating on her paradoxes. It was a bit of a paradox, she ruminated, that she was so darned obsessed with Jonathan yet sometimes so wretched to him and so afraid.

RoseEllen stood at the podium waiting for the group of two hundred family therapists to settle down. Despite her low spirits she had managed to immerse herself in the task at hand and come up with a thorough and well-planned presentation. With slippery hands she adjusted the microphone and scratched her nose. She cleared her throat. The murmurings stopped and the audience, mostly men, gave her their attention. She looked out over the sea of faces and thought for a dizzying moment that she ought to be home watching television and what was she doing here? She prayed that she wouldn't make a fool of herself, and if she did that no one, as was the custom in the olden days of vaudeville, had brought a bag of rotten tomatoes with which to pelt her.

"Good evening, ladies and gentlemen," she started in a quavery voice. "As you know, the topic today will be paradox therapy and the language of neurosis. People, in

100

general, and not only our clients, have a stubborn streak. They will behave in paradoxical ways, often doing what is contrary to their best interests or the opposite of what they are told. With such patients traditional support therapy often does not work. A deliberate attempt to fall asleep at night will keep most people awake. The more a person tries to forgo sweets the more he will crave them. And the more you tell someone to be happy, the more you can be assured that the person will be depressed. How can these paradoxes be used in therapy?"

Warming up to her subject matter, RoseEllen felt her voice grow in strength and swell in volume. She ceased to notice the low rumble of conversation which had started after her "good evening" between two of the less polite members of her audience. She traced the origins of this type of therapy, explained it theoretically and gave several examples of how it could be used practically. She told of a well-known case where paradox therapy had succeeded where all other forms of therapeutic intervention had failed. A severely depressed woman had told her therapist that he was her last hope and if he didn't cure her in three months she would commit suicide. Instead of trying to talk her out of her depression the therapist entered her fantasy. He told her that since she had so little time left she might as well enjoy it and do the things she had always wanted to do but couldn't. First of all, since she was unkempt, he advised her to go to a beauty parlor and get a new hairstyle and new makeup. Then he advised her to spend her remaining money, which she had been too frugal to spend, on new clothes and gourmet foods, on theater and travel. If she had only three months, he urged, she might as well enjoy herself for once. "Be daring!" he had advised. "Talk to people, meet them. If they don't like you it won't matter anyway since you won't be around much longer." The woman gradually began to enjoy living. She began to resent the therapist for what she interpreted as his encouragement of her suicide plan and, almost as if to spite him, she became a happy, well-adjusted person.

RoseEllen ended her talk to resounding applause. Unuttered joy bubbled up inside her. She had done it! Now she would have to field questions from the audience—a piece of cake, given this reception. She was wrong.

The first questioner was a round-faced, sandy-haired man of indeterminate age. "Your approach, madam, borders on the unethical if not the insane. If that woman had committed suicide that therapist and all of you apologists for this ridiculous method would be guilty of aiding and abetting a homicide. Suicide, as you may know, is against the law."

RoseEllen swallowed her anger. To answer that unfounded accusation while still maintaining her dignity would be no easy trick. She didn't have to.

Jonathan Wood, seated without her knowledge in the back row, had risen to his feet and in a loud voice bellowed a retort. "If you, sir, had listened to the lady's speech instead of rudely carrying on a conversation with your neighbor across the aisle, you would never have asked such a question. The answer is obvious. The therapist is not advocating suicide, but by appearing to accept the patient's assumptions, the therapist gets the patient herself to reject these same assumptions. The therapist controls the situation. Besides, she said that in this case no other approach had worked."

The room was hushed. RoseEllen thought she was hearing things. Could this be the man who had termed her a shrink and told her he had no use for psychology? He was defending what she had said as though he had a personal stake in it. He sounded like the staunchest advocate of paradox therapy she had ever heard! People turned around, wondering who he was. Though it was not good form to attack a questioner personally, no matter how absurd the question, RoseEllen noticed some members of her audience nodding their heads. Apparently not a few of them had been annoyed at the mumbling that had gone on during her presentation.

The other questions were on technical points and easy for RoseEllen to handle. She did so with only half her mind. The other half was racing, trying to figure out how Jonathan had found out where she would be speaking, why he had come, why he had come to her rescue, and how he had managed to speak so authoritatively.

When she left the podium, people milled around her pumping her hand. Smiling graciously she scanned the crowd, searching out Jonathan. Wearing a scholarly-looking Irish tweed jacket with gray flannel pants, he was leaning against the rear door with his arms folded across his chest. He watched the ritual of praise with a proud smile. As soon as she could, she disengaged herself from the crowd.

"Jonathan!"

"I don't have your flowers," he apologized.

"Oh." She laughed, looking at him with shining eyes. "How did you find out where I was speaking?"

"I asked your secretary. He's a very helpful guy. You should give him a raise. You were great up there, a real star."

"Thanks. You were sharp as my co-star. I ought to thank you for that. Why did you do it?" she asked, a smile forming at the corners of her mouth.

"That guy needed a comeuppance. He didn't know what he was talking about. Some junkmen can listen and read better than some psychologists." He held out a copy of the book he was holding. It was Watzlawick's famous work on paradox therapy.

"You read that?" RoseEllen couldn't keep the bewilderment out of her voice.

"Sometimes I get tired of reading wine lists."

She gave an embarrassed laugh, abashed at the thoughts she had been harboring about Jonathan and the things she had said to him.

"I like your suede elbow patches," she commented for lack of anything better to say.

"I'm not really your classic elbow-patch sort of guy. Some men wear them on their pajamas," he joked. "I thought they would be appropriate tonight. You look nice in that suit. I like man-tailored white blouses on"—he paused—"voluptuous women."

RoseEllen flushed, aware of how the middle button pulled when she moved her arms.

Drs. Riley and Lewis approached. "Nice going, Rosey. You son of a gun," Dr. Riley addressed Jonathan. "What are you doing here? No need to answer that," he said with a chuckle. "Dr. Lewis, let me introduce you to Mr. Wood, the Mr. Wood I was telling you about the other night."

"Besmirching my good name?" Jonathan asked amusedly.

Dr. Riley laughed. "Now Rosey, whatever else you do, don't let this fellow talk you into any real estate deals. Romance"—he giggled in a high-pitched way she never would have expected—"is one thing. Business is another."

RoseEllen blanched. She didn't want to think about that condo thing right now. Dr. Lewis smiled benignly.

She could almost hear the buzz of gossip that would go on after they left. It was rather unusual, she had to admit, to be defended professionally by one's "friend"—or lover. She startled at the thought. Lover. She supposed he would become her lover. But did she love him?

"So you're a real estate developer?" Dr. Lewis interjected.

"No, I'm a junkman," Jonathan replied with equanimity.

RoseEllen stifled her laughter. She was beginning to understand Jonathan and the pleasure he took in bringing people, especially stuffy people, up short. She thought that if he were a physician he would call himself a plumber and if he were a general he would call himself a soldier. What was he really?

"I see," Dr. Lewis answered, not really seeing at all. He frowned at RoseEllen.

She thought that her mental health in having chosen so unsuitable a companion would be the subject of many a conversation tonight. That was all right with her. At least let them gossip about someone they knew. Placido Domingo was someone they only read about or heard on a stage. She clenched her fists. Here she went, being judgmental again. Why was she sure they would gossip about her and Jonathan? Because she knew this world, she answered her own question. If a man didn't have letters after his name, PhD or MD or at least MS, he didn't quite come up to par. Too bad. Jonathan Wood, JM, was the most beautiful man she had ever set eyes on . . . and considerate, and . . .

"Let's go." Jonathan broke into her thoughts.

"Where?"

"I'm hungry. This heavy intellectual atmosphere has given me an appetite."

"I don't think I should leave yet. There's another speaker after the recess. It wouldn't be polite," she offered halfheartedly.

"Come on. You can read the article later." He pushed her toward the door.

"Well, okay. I am ravenous, if the truth be known."

"Dr. Riley." He nodded. "Nice meeting you, Dr. Lewis."

"Mr. Wood," they chorused.

Jonathan ushered her into the low-slung Porsche.

"I have my car here," she remembered.

"You can get it later." Jonathan smiled at her as he pressed in his lighter and pulled a gold-tipped cigarette out of a new pack.

"So my hypnosis didn't work at all. I realize it was a big joke to you, but even so I thought I might have had some effect."

"You did. I'm completely under your spell." He put the cigarette away.

"How about throwing out the pack?"

"You're a very demanding woman." He put it in the glove compartment and locked it. "Is that good enough?"

"Of course not. You've got the key!" She laughed.

His eyes darted briefly over her face before he started the car. His hands, large, sinewy, and graceful, rested lightly on the steering wheel of the well-tuned automobile. It was odd, RoseEllen fretted, how she never tired of watching his hands. Despite the unusually heavy evening traffic he weaved in and out of Broad Street's clogged lanes and headed from the north Philadelphia conference hall to center city.

She breathed deeply of the smells of Jonathan's car and of Jonathan. They were a mixture of new car scent, tanned leather from the seats, and a musky, slightly spicy after-shave which she couldn't place but which smelled expensive. She wore no perfume and just hoped that the sweater she had brought along against summer night breezes didn't reek of mothballs. She marveled at the sensations which were hers tonight. Back in Gladfeldter Hall, behind the podium, she had felt a feeling of power, a feeling that she could control her audience. It was a heady sensation. Power aside, feminism aside, she thought now with a hint of mournfulness, that feeling did not compare in intensity to the delicious anticipation of riding into the night with Jonathan Wood.

Putting on the brake, Jonathan stopped at the red light. He caught her hand in his, and lifting it to his lips, he planted a soft kiss in her palm. Her intake of breath was sharp. She waited a second too long to pull her hand away. Now he knew. She could tell from the dominant way he looked at her.

He took her to Smithwick's Exchange, a bar and grill at the Philadelphia Bourse. A lovely nineteenth-century building with swirls, balustrades, and colonnades, the Bourse once housed a commodities exchange and had recently been renovated to house elegant shops and restaurants. Smithwick's Exchange was paneled in dark wood, was dimly lighted, and according to Jonathan, had some of the city's best oysters.

"It is a little tacky," Jonathan said as he pointed out the commodities board which was on a direct electronic line to the Chicago Board of Trade and which reflected not only the prices of commodities but also all weekend sports scores. "What will you have?"

"The crab cocktail sounds good. To start with at least," she added. She was starving. For the past two days she had been living on grilled cheese sandwiches and Campbell's soup.

When Jonathan gave the order he also requested a bottle of Moët & Chandon.

"I'm used to Great Western. I don't know if my palate will appreciate French champagne," RoseEllen joked.

"You just need some educating," Jonathan grinned.

RoseEllen smiled back.

When the champagne was served, Jonathan lifted his glass to her in a toast. "To RoseEllen, who under no circumstances will accompany me next Saturday to Reading, PA, for an excruciatingly boring auction and who, without any doubt, will not afterward indulge in capricious and sinful activities with yours truly."

Laughingly, RoseEllen lifted her own glass. "To Jonathan, whose mastery of paradox theory though impressive is not sufficient to lure me away." Their laughing, twinkling eyes met across the table.

"You must admit I'm a quick learner," Jonathan said.

"Quicker than I. Tell me about your auction."

"For one thing," he drawled, "it's closed to the public. It's by invitation only."

"How come?"

"It's to keep out the auction addicts who travel from auction to auction trying to bid on everything from cases of barbecue sauce to pink flamingo lawn ornaments."

"I take it then," she offered, "that it's more than old issues of *National Geographic* and tea kettles that are auctioned off."

"You might figure on that." He laughed easily.

"Don't just sit there laughing," she prodded. "Tell me."

108

"Why do you want to know? You're not coming."

"I'm interested," she replied defensively.

"Train or ship cargoes that, for one reason or another, are abandoned or have become burdensome for the owners are auctioned off. They can be anything from padded bras to a ton of copper. We could have a factory owner who has to liquidate the contents of a warehouse or perhaps a few thousand bushels of wheat that a farmer wants to get rid of quickly. Then we'll have an old building or a couple of French antiques. You don't know till you get there. And you don't know if you'll be dealing in big bucks or megabucks."

"I suppose you really have to know what you're doing," she remarked.

"It helps."

RoseEllen cleared her throat. "Next Saturday just isn't good for me. It sounds great but I have a busy week at the office and I have an appointment to get my hair cut on Saturday." *And,* she added silently to herself, *I have to steal myself against your damned charm!*

"You're absolutely right." He nodded emphatically. "You couldn't let your hair go! There's nothing more crucial to a woman than well-cut hair, cut exactly at the right moment. By all means get it cut."

RoseEllen felt her skin prickle. He was doing it again—using her paradoxical approach against her. And this time he was doing it well. He knew that she knew that her excuses sounded hopelessly feeble. She felt like an idiot.

"And I have to repot some plants and pick up a couple of things for the apartment. I'll never get everything done this week. I need a lamp and I would love to get one of those lacquered Chinese chests if I can find a bargain and

109

I do my grocery shopping on Saturdays." Her words tumbled out one against the other.

"You *do* have a lot to do next week!" he agreed wholeheartedly. "Grocery shopping is something one should *never* put off. The lamp is essential also. Reading by candlelight went out with Ben Franklin. And as for lacquered Chinese chests—if you need one, you need one. There's no two ways about it. They only sell them on the third Saturday of each month so if you miss out next week you might as well forget it! And your plants! I don't know what you're doing sitting here. You should be home repotting right now. And talking to them and playing classical music. Philodendron particularly like Mozart, I hear. And that rubber plant I gave you—well, that one likes Dvorak. So if you don't have the New World Symphony you had better stop at a record store on your way home. I don't want you putting off that repotting one more day or I might report you to the plant abuse hot line."

"Okay." She sighed resignedly. "What time do you want me to be ready on Saturday?"

Their smiles turned to chuckles which turned to guffaws which turned to gales of laughter. The patrons in the restaurant, the waiters, the maitre d', all turned around to see what the striking couple in the back thought was so hilarious.

"Will you come home with me tonight?" he asked softly.

"Yes, I will," she answered without hesitation. Her heart was thudding so loudly she almost didn't notice the twenty-dollar bill he had tossed on the table for the waiter. She had never known anybody who left twenty-dollar tips for what couldn't have been more than a fifty-dollar check.

His eyes were wide and soulful, glinting amber and reminding her of liquid gold. He stood before her, his hands circling her waist, as her arms went around his neck. For a moment he held her away from him as he looked into her face. A small smile played upon his lips. Drawing her closer then, he bent his head to kiss her. She saw his face looming larger and nothing existed except Jonathan and the thrill of abandon that was searing through her. His lips were moist, his mouth eager. His tongue darted aggressively as he probed, explored, tasted her. The intimate kisses induced warm, exciting twinges deep within her. Shyly at first she answered his kisses. With her small, eager tongue, she tasted his lips and then the moist cavern of his mouth.

"Oh, Jonathan," she sighed, suddenly inarticulate from the rush of her emotions.

"I'm glad you came," he said gruffly.

Suddenly she was swept up into his arms and he was carrying her to the bedroom. With one hand he pulled off the spread and dropped it to the floor. He laid her gently on the smooth blue sheets. He sat down beside her and gently touched her cheek.

"RoseEllen Robbins, do you know what you're doing?"

"I do," she whispered and caught his hair-roughened hand and brought it to her lips.

He moved his hand caressingly over her chin, her throat, her breasts. His eyes stared into hers and he stood to unbutton his shirt. With slow deliberateness he undid his cuffs and then the front of the shirt. RoseEllen raised her hand as if to touch the wide expanse of chest but he was not near enough to her. Greedily she stared at him. When he divested himself of his pants she saw that his legs, his buttocks, were no less beautifully muscled than his torso. He sat beside her and watched as she unbuttoned her blouse. He unfastened her bra. RoseEllen was glad she had worn her new bra for she knew that the way the beige lace barely covered the nipples emphasized the delicate creaminess of her skin tones. She shifted to help him with her skirt and panties, but realized that he needed no assistance.

"So beautiful, so beautiful," he breathed as he beheld her naked.

Her own eyes followed his as they traced a searing path from her rosebud nipples which had stiffened at his first glance to the slightly rounded swell of her belly to the firm, tanned thighs and slender legs. No man had ever looked at her this way. She could tell from the tender, awestruck expression in his eyes that she pleased him. She felt no shame, just a little modesty that he had not extinguished the lamp, and that everything about her, down to the tiny mole at the side of her belly button, was open to his examination.

"Won't you turn off the light?"

"No. I want to see the way you quiver at my touch and turn so warmly pink." He winked.

With his hands and lips he traced the same path that his eyes had blazed. She trembled. When he gently parted her legs to kiss the soft, inner skin of her thighs she could no longer restrain her moans of pleasure.

"Oh Jonathan, now . . ."

Refusing to acknowledge the urgency of her desire he slowly stroked her. He put both hands on her hips and then moved them languorously up and down her body. She bit into his shoulder, tasting the faint saltiness of his skin. Lifting one leg, he kissed the back of her thigh and knee. RoseEllen thought she wouldn't survive this on-slaught of her senses. What was this power he possessed, this junkman, this Jonathan Wood? She touched his shoulders, she kneaded his back, and then tentatively moved her hands down to touch him intimately.

Jonathan groaned, and swinging her smooth length on top of him he brushed her hair back with one hand and with the other he pressed her against him. Her breasts, flattened against the rough hair of his chest, were alive with sensation. Her nipples seemed to have a life of their own. She was soft, vulnerable, and yielding against him. As she had wanted nothing before she wanted to open herself to this man, to give him everything she had to give.

He kept one hand in her hair, the other he let rest on her hip. Even with the slight pull she felt in her scalp, which increased as she moved, she rubbed herself slowly against him, insinuating her femininity into his every pore. He kissed her, and she answered his kisses as if they provided the only nourishment to a starving soul.

Rolling her over, Jonathan looked and smilingly de-manded, "Tell me how much you want me. I want to hear it from your lips."

"I want you. I want you now, Jonathan." She stopped, not wanting to talk or think anymore.

Though she tensed, the exquisite sweetness he brought her soon drained away her apprehension. Jonathan was gentle yet demanding, patient yet forceful. He varied the rhythm of his lovemaking; its pace was sometimes fren-zied, sometimes maddeningly slow. She knew he was exer-cising supreme control by the way the veins stood out so angrily in his muscled neck. Once, when she thought that she could wait no longer, that she would explode in rap-ture, the phone rang. With his lips glued to hers, Jonathan

113

groped to lift the receiver off the hook and then to hang up without bothering to find out who was on the other end. Having broken the phone connection he knocked the phone off the night table with a cool deliberateness in order to forestall any further interruptions.

"Weren't you even curious?" RoseEllen asked.

"Nothing could be more interesting than what I have here," he rasped.

She held his face in both her hands then and looked into his eyes, wanting to live in their dark, brooding depths.

Taking one of her hands from his cheek he raised it back over her head and with their hands clasped they rose to a crescendo of ecstasy. This time there was no holding back the explosion when it came. It came in waves again and again, taking her breath away. Her hand gripped his tightly in an achingly simple gesture of trust as he carried her away to a land of pure sensation. A moan slipped from her throat and she felt him brushing his lips against eyelashes that were wet from tears. The intimacy and violence of their blissful release had left her feeling shaken. She was still trembling when he slipped from between her legs. When he picked up her hand to kiss her palm she felt an unutterable tenderness for him and she bit her lips to keep from saying words she might regret tomorrow.

"Your lips are swollen," he uttered softly. He passed his forefinger gently over them.

With his tongue he stemmed the rivulet of perspiration that had formed between and under her breasts. With his hands he pushed the white globes together, and burying his face between the tender flesh he kissed her nipples reverently. Before she knew it a familiar fire was once again raging inside her and she felt herself pushing against him with a primitive female urgency. This time their lovemaking was slower, less insistent. She wrapped her legs around him and they moved together in perfect sync. When it was over he smiled at her and if she wanted she could have read a million words into his expression. She willed herself to look away for suddenly she felt afraid. Her emotions were too raw, too vulnerable.

"You're lovely," he breathed.

"Is that why you wanted me, because you like the way I look?"

"That's part of it," he answered truthfully, "although yours is a deeper kind of beauty. When you're old you'll still be gorgeous. The structure is there; the high cheekbones, the wide, sensuous mouth, the light in your eyes, the intelligence."

"I think I'm getting hungry again," she faltered in an attempt at levity.

"I have just the thing." Swinging his legs over the side of the bed, he walked naked to the kitchen.

Watching his retreating form she thought it amazing that still he looked cool and unruffled. She jumped up, picked up her clothes from the floor, and headed for the bathroom and a quick shower.

When she returned fully dressed, he was lying on the bed wearing a pair of jeans. A big Lucite bowl of popcorn rested on his chest. On the night table beside him were two fluted glasses and a bottle of good champagne which he unceremoniously uncorked.

"Why are you dressed?" he asked as he handed her a full glass. "You can wear one of my T-shirts to sleep."

"I can't stay." She stuffed a handful of popcorn into her mouth so she wouldn't have to elaborate. She didn't know what she could say. Telling him she was afraid was no reason. And what was she afraid of? Too much pleasure?

115

The pain that was a part of all happiness? Endings? Or herself? What *was* she afraid of?

From the massive mahogany chest that took up almost one whole wall of his bedroom, Jonathan ignored her refusal and took out a long green-and-white Philadelphia Eagles T-shirt. "This will be comfortable for you."

Wordlessly, RoseEllen took it and stood up to undress again.

When late that night she finally fell asleep it was with her head against Jonathan's chest and her arms on top of his.


With RoseEllen back at work the next week and with Jonathan preoccupied with his business, they saw each other only twice before the Saturday of the auction. He took her to the racetrack one evening, and she took him to the Barnes Foundation. She had never been to the racetrack before, had thought she would hate it. It turned out that she shouted with the rest of the crowd as the horses approached the finish line. It was *fun* losing twenty dollars.

Jonathan had protested loudly about the Barnes Foundation, a private collection of priceless paintings open to a limited public on special days. He disliked Impressionist paintings, he had told her. They were too soppy and sentimental. He wound up buying a dozen art postcards in the Foundation gift shop.

It struck her with increasing frequency that she hadn't bargained for the intensity of this relationship. Where, at the beginning, she had felt herself to be the more sophisticated one, it appeared to her now that he possessed a great deal more savvy than she. Though he had told her more about himself he was still fundamentally unfamiliar. He wasn't safe. Sometimes she felt a cold blast of uncertainty knifing through her. Her carefully ordered life didn't seem to be all hers anymore.

# CHAPTER SEVEN

RoseEllen reached out her arm to stop the jangling of her alarm clock. She groaned. It couldn't be five thirty already. She felt as if she had just fallen asleep. She opened one eye. The alarm clock wasn't wrong. Groggily she dragged herself out of bed and into the kitchen, where she lit a flame under the pot of coffee she had had the foresight to prepare the night before. She lifted the shade of her kitchen window to the darkness outside, then pulled it down again.

To say she was not an early morning person would not be an overstatement, she thought. Her body was programmed to function at nine o'clock and not a minute before. Jonathan was picking her up in half an hour and he had told her that she better not be late. The trip to Reading would take at least an hour and a half and the auction began at nine sharp. Well, she could have slept in for at least another hour and they still would have been on time. Why hadn't she thought of that last night when there was still time to do something about it? She wondered briefly if he was the type of compulsive person who had to get places early, the type to arrive at airports two hours before the plane was scheduled to depart or at movie theaters in time to cool their heels for forty minutes before the show began.

She gulped her coffee. It had that bitter taste of coffee brewed the day before. She shrugged, too sleepy to care. After laying her nightgown on the bed she stumbled into the shower. The combination of cool water and caffeine began working and she started to feel human. She dressed with care, choosing a stylishly short, slightly full, black cotton skirt with a striped turquoise-and-black shirt. She pulled on turquoise tinted panty hose and her new black pumps. Her reflection in the mirror satisfied her. She was well put together, svelte; her legs looked superb, and her face had that gaunt, haunted look that many of the world's most glamorous women strive for through the judicious use of makeup. RoseEllen, with her high cheekbones, hollows in her cheeks, and large, luminous eyes, came by it naturally. Her chestnut hair gleamed. RoseEllen thought that perhaps she ought to reconsider the blunt, chinlength haircut she had thought about. The only thing RoseEllen would change if she could was the size of her breasts. They were slightly too large, she thought, for her slender frame.

When Jonathan rang the downstairs buzzer she was ready. She took a quick look around, making sure that the stove was off, the shower had stopped dripping, and she had her keys and money.

"Good morning," she called as she slid into the bucket seat. She leaned over to plant a kiss on his cheek.

"You look great," he answered. "Predawn agrees with you."

"The last time I was up and around this early was when I was in Girl Scout camp. I only went for one year. Even when I was twelve I didn't believe that rise and shine and cold baked beans and sleeping bags were fun."

"Not even sleeping bags?" he asked, grinning.

"No. I always felt like the odd one out because I secretly thought the best part about Girl Scouts was the cookies."

"I can't picture you as a child," he said thoughtfully.

"It seems that you must have always been balanced and, well, no-nonsense."

"So you think I'm a no-nonsense person?"

"Yep. The kind of woman who doesn't get bogged down in details or gossip. You see the big picture. You could do with a little immaturity!" He grinned. "Sometimes you look so serious that I think the best gift I could buy for you would be a pair of bifocals to wear on a velvet string around your neck."

"I refuse to be offended by that remark!" She laughed.

As they talked Jonathan nosed the car onto the Schuylkill Espressway, called the Surekill Expressway by some drivers because of all the potholes and lanes which appeared and disappeared without warning. The road, save for a few trucks, was empty. Jonathan made good time. When he turned onto the Pennsylvania Turnpike he greeted the tolltaker with a cheery good morning and a comment about the beautiful weather in store. Looking surprised, the woman answered in kind.

"You're friendly. That's refreshing," RoseEllen remarked.

"I don't like when I see people treating tollbooth workers, telephone operators, and the like as if they were automatons. Too many people act as if behaving courteously costs them something."

Like the expressway, the turnpike was empty for long stretches, and Jonathan pressed the accelerator almost to the floor.

When the speedometer hit eighty, RoseEllen, who had been gripping the seat, spoke. "You're going to get a ticket."

"No, I won't."

"Don't you think you're going a little too fast?" she suggested dryly.

"Are you afraid?" He let up slightly on the gas pedal.

RoseEllen, whose knuckles were white, avoided answering his question directly. "I think you're a candidate for Judge McIntyre's speeding program. I'll give you a reduced rate."

"Don't worry. I've never had an accident. Anyway, we're getting off at the next exit. We can take back roads the rest of the way. Pennsylvania Dutch country starts around here and we can enjoy some unforgettable scenery."

"My hometown isn't too far from here," RoseEllen pointed out flatly. "That's given me enough unforgettable scenery to last a lifetime."

"Didn't you like it there?"

"It was all right. Occasionally I go back to see my family and friends. But Dillsburg is one of those towns where you can only be one of two things—good or bad. And if you were bad and you skinned your knees or caught the sniffles, it was because you were being 'punished.' You always got what you deserved," she finished resignedly.

Jonathan laughed. "And what were you—good or bad?"

"What do you think?" She grimaced. "I was as good as gold. What a burden that was. Even now when I get sick, somewhere in the back of my mind I believe it's because I was rude or inconsiderate or didn't give enough to UNICEF when they came around."

Jonathan squeezed her knee. "Your problem is that there's a very naughty girl hiding in there somewhere behind that beautiful, clean-scrubbed face. I'm helping to set her free, I think."

"Oh Jonathan!" She pushed his hand away and felt herself redden. "It serves me right for telling you anything!"

His hand was back but this time it slid all the way up her thigh. It was hot and rough against the cool silkiness of her hose. The intensity with which her body responded to his touch jolted her. She wanted to tell him to pull over to the side; she wanted to lie back and urge him on. With both hands this time she pushed him away, crossed her legs, and moved against the door. Her heart was hammering against the thin material of her shirt. It was positively indecent to feel this way at seventy miles an hour on the turnpike!

"Are you hungry?" Jonathan asked with equanimity.

"Starved, now that I think about it," she replied in carefully measured tones.

"There's a nice little inn not far from here." He headed for the exit ramp and turned down a winding road just off the highway.

The inn was small, spare, and scrupulously clean, with no decorations. The shiny oak floor and the muslin curtains hanging at the windows emphasized the stark simplicity of the dining room. It was crowded with local folk, Amish men in their white shirts and black suits and hats looking just as they did two hundred years ago, a milkman, and a couple of families with their pigtailed and cowlicked broods.

Jonathan headed for the only empty table, in the far corner of the room.

RoseEllen was glad for that. She didn't want to be stared at. Nonetheless, some of the people at the tables craned their necks to look at her and Jonathan. With all her carefully cultivated poise, she still felt that she ought to be wearing a big red *A*. Of course she was being silly. She wasn't an adulteress and these days it was very normal for two unmarried people to have breakfast together. Still, she took care to keep her ringless left hand carefully hidden in her lap.

She was so deeply involved in her thoughts that she hadn't even noticed when Jonathan began talking to one of the Amish men seated at the next table. He was giving him advice on a new ball bearing for his buggy. The Amish didn't drive cars, preferring to follow the old ways. The man thanked Jonathan earnestly. The waitress stood waiting to take their order. Jonathan ordered for both of them: eggs, waffles, scrapple, and coffee.

RoseEllen wrinkled her nose. "*You* are going to eat my scrapple. I intend to die without ever tasting the stuff." The mere thought of scrapple, the highly spiced, fried by-products of pork, made her ill.

"That's certainly an ambitious goal." Jonathan winked. "I never knew you were finicky about food."

"I'm not but I have my limits. I'll eat snails, I'll eat kidneys, but scrapple—forget it!"

With a resigned shrug, Jonathan signaled the waitress. "Hold the scrapple on my wife's order, please."

"Why did you say that?" RoseEllen whispered.

"I think I know you well enough to know what you're feeling."

"Maybe *you* should be the psychologist." RoseEllen lapsed into silence, uncomfortable with herself. Before Jonathan, she had almost always been in control of her life. Now she seemed spineless. It was he who handled everything with ease, both people and situations. Nothing could shake his composure. He handled her; he handled tollbooth workers; he handled Amish farmers.

The food came, mountains of it. The coffee was fresh, the eggs tasted as if the hen had just laid them, the waffles were crisp. Jonathan finished everything on his plate and called for a slice of shoofly pie. RoseEllen ate half of her eggs but just a bite of her waffles.

"Don't you like it?" he asked.

"It's delicious. But I have to watch what I eat. I put weight on easily."

"I'd like to see you a little fuller." He puffed his cheeks to illustrate.

"No, you wouldn't."

"You're not one of those women obsessed by the tyranny of skinniness, are you?" he asked suspiciously.

"Not really. I usually eat what I want. I'm lucky that what I want is usually cottage cheese and dry toast for breakfast." She laughed. "I will have more coffee though." She glanced at her watch. "Do we have enough time?"

"If you drink fast."

RoseEllen did. Jonathan paid the bill, leaving a five-dollar tip, which on a seven-dollar bill made RoseEllen feel as if her eyes would pop. Whenever she dined out, she was scrupulously careful to leave not a penny more nor less than the acceptable fifteen percent.

Though he had hurried her in the restaurant, Jonathan drove at a leisurely pace, past well-kept Pennsylvania Dutch farms with their barns decorated with hex signs, past horses and buggies, past quaint towns bearing the incredible names of Intercourse and Blue Ball, across covered wooden bridges and along bubbling creeks.

The auction was being held in a hall in the center of Reading. When they arrived it was almost full. She looked around. She was the only woman present. Most of the men, seated on cushiony vinyl chairs, were conservatively dressed in vested suits. Jonathan wore his taupe blazer and cream-colored slacks with a panache equaled by none. As he led her to seats in the front row that had apparently been saved for them, she could not help but notice how many auctiongoers greeted him. He was well known here.

The low hum in the room was immediately broken off as the auctioneer stepped to the stage. There went another misconception. She had expected the hall to be a large, drafty barn, the seats to be metal folding chairs, and the auctioneer to have slicked-down hair, a handlebar mustache, blue jeans, a belt with a big silver buckle, and maybe even spurs on his boots. This auctioneer looked like a partner in a stock brokerage firm.

When the bidding began RoseEllen sat transfixed. The first item, a warehouse full of desks, went quickly. She hadn't even heard anyone bidding before it was sold for "fifty G's."

"What happened?" she asked.

"The bidding is done with signals. Make sure you don't scratch your ear!"

"Despite what you told me about this last week I still expected this to be a 'Do I hear five? Do I hear ten? Do I hear fifteen? Sold to the man with the torn undershirt!' type of thing," she whispered back.

Jonathan chucked her under the chin in a brotherly fashion.

"A good auctioneer is very, very sharp. And this fellow is good. He knows values, how to get a bid going, and how to sell the impossible to a very sharp group. He's not so much a showman as a businessman." Jonathan went back to studying the sheet of paper which he had pulled from his wallet.

"Like you," she uttered softly.

Jonathan spent the next half hour without even raising an eyebrow. Men sauntered over to him occasionally to whisper things in his ear. He always shook his head no. Without appearing to, she watched him. He was utterly absorbed in what was going on around him. His forehead was furrowed, his lips were drawn in a straight, immutable line, and his eyes gleamed with concentration. Once a man who was introduced to her as Roland and another who was called Liam tried in hoarse whispers to convince Jonathan to enter into a temporary consortium with them on a copper deal that was next on the agenda. Jonathan was firm in his refusal, patiently explaining to them that copper was a poor risk right now at the price he wagered the auctioneer was going to open at. Conditions in Zambia, with the labor unrest and strikes in the mines settled, and in Zimbabwe, with the popular government in power, indicated that the market would soon be flooded with copper at low prices, he told them.

RoseEllen gulped audibly. Some junkman he was. International financier was more like it!

Almost before she could close her mouth, which had fallen unbecomingly open, Jonathan had successfully bid on a shipment of drill bits which, he explained, he would export to South American oil rigs; on half a ton of silicon salts, which would be used to make computer chips; and on a warehouse full of suspenders.

"Suspenders? Isn't . . . that . . . a bit risky?" she asked.

"A little. I could lose my shirt in this business but I won't lose my pants!"

Cocking her head RoseEllen acknowledged the remark with pursed lips and an exaggerated fluttering of eyelashes.

"Do you mind waiting here while I make arrangements for delivery?" he asked solicitously.

"Not at all."

He had hardly left his seat when Jonathan was surrounded by businessmen slapping him on the back, shaking his hand, and one or two who spoke to him in low tones without looking him in the eye. Jonathan breezily extricated himself from the group to talk with the auctioneer.

How much savoir faire he had, she thought. How sharp he was. There was something about the lines of his mouth, hard, etched lines which made it clear to the world that he was not a man to be taken lightly. No one could cheat him. A shiver went up and down her spine. But maybe, the other voice at the back of her mind insisted, he was too savvy, too much the wheeler-dealer. There was that condo business she had heard about, an unsavory affair from what she could glean. And he *had* given her the proverbial snow job. Jonathan Wood was a man who went after what he wanted. She had put up a classic fight— catch me if you can—and he had won. It was as simple as that. He was so damn charming, that was the trouble. And so effective. But Jonathan Wood was not to be trusted. He went around calling himself a junkman. He was no more a junkman than she. He had told her flatly that he had no use for psychology, except when it served his own purposes. Jonathan was full of contradictions. She was seeing that clearly now.

Since she had been back at work her life had seemed divided in two. There was the serious RoseEllen Robbins who was respected and competent. And there was the RoseEllen Robbins who lived each moment as if she only had that moment. It had been lovely the week before with

Jonathan. She had still been on vacation then, and it had been a lark. Jonathan too would soon come to that conclusion. She really wasn't in his league. Intrigued by her bearing, her looks, and her job, he would discover that despite it all she was a simple, small-town girl who lived in the big city. So, she told herself, it had been nothing more than a vacation romance. It shouldn't be prolonged. Instead of taking place at the Club Med in Guadeloupe or Martinique, it had taken place in good old Philadelphia. Like all vacation flings it meant no more than a good time—a fling in the sun—or the smog.

When Jonathan returned, it was to a RoseEllen who sat primly with arms folded across her chest and a belligerent look in her eye.

"Bored? I'm sorry I took so long. I ran into a couple of snags."

"That's all right. I'm sorry you're having a problem." She stood up and walked out with him to the car.

"There's some difficulty in specifications for the drill bits and in getting the delivery date of the silicon salts to my warehouse."

"You have a warehouse?" she asked incredulously.

"Three of them. They're small though."

"Three small warehouses," she repeated. "Not bad for a junkman."

As they reached the curb where Jonathan's Porsche sat, RoseEllen looked at him levelly. "I hate to pierce your armor but I want to know. Why do you call yourself a junkman?"

Jonathan winced and laughed. "I knew we'd get to that sooner or later. Because, my esteemed shrink, if there's one thing I detest it's pretentiousness. If somebody is going to like me it's not going to be on the strength of what

128

I call myself but what I am. Doctor, lawyer, or Indian chief are artificial distinctions separating people. I don't need them and I don't usually care for people who do." He opened the car door for her.

As RoseEllen sat back in the soft leather she was not surprised. It was a given that he would have a good answer. Jonathan was never at a loss for words.

As the car picked up speed a small knot of despair which had formed in RoseEllen's stomach grew. She didn't know where it came from or where it would take her. She was twenty-eight. She was single. She had never had a successful, long-term relationship. There had always been something not quite right about the men. The pattern was repeating itself. She was involved with a man, whatever his profession, who was not right for her. They were too different. He had probably never done a charitable act in his life. His behavior was outrageous and anyway there was a good chance that with her prissiness (yes, it was true) he would soon tire of her. She did have a way of messing things up. Sometimes she imagined a little demon somewhere in her mind forcing her to say or do things that would ruin a relationship. So Jonathan Wood wasn't Mr. Perfect. Mr. Perfect didn't exist. What was that old cliché? Physician, heal thyself. But did she want to?

Flipping the buttons of his car radio Jonathan chose some soothing music. Once again, he chose meandering back roads where the countryside was bucolic and lush.

"Pennsylvania is a beautiful state," he muttered, "and vastly underrated by the rest of the country."

"It is," she agreed. "It's the kind of natural beauty that wouldn't come across on a postcard, though. It would look unrealistic. Maybe that's why it's underrated. It's so green it's almost sweet." RoseEllen was relieved at the impersonal turn the conversation had taken and hoped that it would continue in this vein until they arrived back in Philadelphia. She had some hard thinking to do.

"Yes, waterfalls and mountains might make better subjects for postcards," Jonathan added, "but right now I'm not interested in postcards. I'm interested in RoseEllen Robbins. Let's spend the night here. We can find an inn or a farm that rents out rooms."

So much for impersonal, she thought wryly. "I don't think so."

"Why not?"

What should she say? she wondered frantically. Because I'm getting too involved? *Because I'm afraid for my sanity? Because this will never work? Because I don't know who you really are or who I really am but anyway we're too different?* No, she wasn't up to an out-and-out confrontation.

"Because"—she hesitated—"I don't have my toothbrush."

Braking so hard the tires screeched, Jonathan made a tight U-turn and headed in the opposite direction. He stopped in front of a small general store that was half a mile back.

"Be right out," he said as he dashed into the store.

As good as his word he returned in a matter of seconds, not nearly enough time for RoseEllen to untangle her thoughts. He threw a paper bag on her lap. She didn't have to look to know what it contained but she did. There were two brand-new red toothbrushes, a tube of Colgate, baby powder, Jergen's hand lotion, and a disposable razor.

"The selection wasn't too big," he apologized.

The short silence was charged.

"Toothpaste and red toothbrushes are fine but I'm still

not going," she said through gritted teeth. She crossed her legs and folded her hands to keep him from seeing that her whole body was shaking.

"You're not going to make me use paradox therapy on you again, are you? At this rate, I'll soon be a certified therapist." Though the words were light he ground them out between clenched teeth and the sneer in his voice was perceptible.

"I don't want you to use anything on me. I just want to go home. Thank you for taking me to the auction but that's all I agreed to. You didn't tell me extracurricular activities were included in the price of admission," she spat out.

"I think you might have suspected," he answered blandly. "We *are* past the peck-on-the-cheek stage. You know what your problem is? I'll tell you. You're a frightened, insecure, rather rigid woman who pretends to be confident and detached and you're falling in love with me and you're scared to death."

A bomb felt like it was exploding in her head. She was left speechless. She could feel the blood draining from her face and fingers. So that's what he thought of her. She forced herself to answer.

"Your problem is you're a pompous ass!"

"My problem," he corrected her, "is that I'm also scared to death. For thirty-two years I've remained shackle-free."

"If I have anything to do with it it'll last another thirty-two," she vowed.

"Come on," he cajoled.

Pulling the car over to the side of the road, where he stopped it, he reached a strong hand out to her. She shrank back. With an impatient sigh, he got out, walked around to her door, opened it, and pulled her out and to her feet. Her eyes were wide and her mouth slightly parted with wonder as he gravely cradled her face in his hands. He tilted her chin up so that their eyes met. What he'd said and what she saw in his eyes was too much for her to bear. She closed her eyes as his arms moved to encircle her. She swayed against him, powerless to fight him anymore, powerless against the waves of longing that swept through her at his slightest touch. His kiss started softly, tracing the outline of her jaw to her eyelashes, planting small tantalizing kisses on her neck, exploring the region behind her ears. When he sought her mouth, his kiss became so persuasive, the rhythmic flickering of his tongue so ardent, that she could not still her own desire.

She slipped her arms around the hard muscles of his neck, feeling nothing but the tender torment of her need. She was tinglingly conscious of the length of his body pressed firmly against the length of hers. He knew her too well. He was right in everything he had said. He knew that only he could wrest this reaction from her and that knowledge made her hate him just a little. A passing car honked at them. Pulling away she was in time to see its teenage passengers sending them jubilant arm signals.

"We'd better go," she whispered.

"Why? They're just jealous," he muttered as he nuzzled her neck.

"We're in a public place. That does seem to be your thing, though." She laughed, remembering the escapade in the fountain.

"Come with me." He motioned toward the high field of wheat beside them.

"Splendor in the wheat," she said with an ironic self-consciousness.

132

"You have another problem," he said brusquely. "You don't know when to keep quiet." As they walked he moved his hand caressingly up and around her neck. "Sometimes I don't know whether I want to stroke this white flesh or pinch it."

Lifting her head back against his hand she looked at him deliberately, challengingly, exposing the full column of her neck to him, daring him to make good his words. With a groan he lowered his head to her neck, pressing lips against cool skin. They had reached the wheatfield and, with their lips seeking each other's, they lowered themselves to the soft ground. RoseEllen, as she explored his mouth with the tip of her tongue, delighted in his kisses that rained down upon her face and her lips. She told herself that it would go no further. Still, the feel of his body against hers, of his leg stretched between her legs, of their ankles locking, was becoming too much for her. She was unprepared for the sweet warmth which surged through her body.

Feeling her resolve fading she pushed Jonathan back a little, saying, "Let's not here." Stiffening imperceptibly, Jonathan lay back with his arms behind his head, a long filament of wheat jutting out of the corner of his mouth. They lay there for a few minutes inhaling the pungent, fertile aroma of the earth. Part of her felt at peace and content, the other part self-critical and self-conscious as always. Jonathan took the wheat from his mouth and began slowly caressing her arms, her neck and breasts. Moving onto his side he stretched out alongside her again as they gently kissed. This time she wrapped her arms around his neck and they slowly undulated to the rhythm of the breeze-driven wheat swaying above them.

Feeling his hand at the base of her back pulling her

toward him, she stopped thinking and let herself revel in the sensations of her body. As Jonathan rolled on top of her, RoseEllen's legs spread naturally. Jonathan's hands and mouth worshipped her face. Her faint perfume, his cologne, and the earthy smells of the wheatfield combined in a timeless ambrosia. She opened her eyes and saw a vein on Jonathan's forehead pulsating.

As he began to unbutton her shirt, a fleeting draft of air cooled her barely perspiring breasts, at the same time adding to her heightened senses and sobering her slightly.

Jonathan smiled. "Splendor in the wheat is right. You're the staff of life."

She smiled languidly as he took his shirt off. When he removed his pants, though, she was assailed by her too-persistent sense of propriety as well as by questions about Jonathan. This was too natural for him and not the right place for her.

Still, when he lay beside her caressing her exposed breasts, gentling the crests with his tongue and his lips, she found herself melting once again. But this time she resisted. She felt in some confused way that she loved, yes, loved him, but . . .

He looked at her penetratingly. "Something wrong?"

"No."

"Then why the hesitancy?"

"Nothing . . ." she stammered.

Just then she heard, seemingly only ten feet away, the clop-clop of a horse's hooves and the peculiar singsong tones of a Pennsylvania Dutch voice. "Easy there, easy there."

Through the stalks she could barely discern a horse and carriage heading toward them. She scrambled for her clothes as Jonathan remonstrated, "He can't see us."

"He might. Besides, I'm . . ."

"What?"

"Jonathan, let's get dressed."

A momentary expression of exasperation passed across his eyes. "If that's the way you want it."

He dressed in a flash. She was still buttoning her blouse when he stood ready, his jacket over one shoulder, whistling an old show tune. As they walked to the car he didn't even look at her. To try and regain a semblance of composure RoseEllen busied herself by brushing bits of wheat and grass from her clothes. Confused and irritated, for what she had done and for what she hadn't done, she thought it absurd that at twenty-eight she should feel like a schoolgirl, like a tease.

The car nosed along at a faster clip than was prudent on the narrow country roads.

"I'll be getting on the turnpike soon," he said after a strained silence. "You should be home in an hour."

The bag full of toiletries sat between them, a silent accusation.

She hadn't said she definitely wouldn't spend the night with him at an inn, though it was clear to both of them that she hadn't wanted to, at least not then and not in that way. Her reasons, such as they were, had nothing to do with any notion of morality, but strangely enough with the love she felt for him. She loved him but wanted to know more about him, to feel more comfortable and natural with him. He was so strange, so direct, not like the academic and therapist types whose motives and values she understood. Underneath his dashing facade, he seemed to be warm and stable and generous, but she wasn't sure. Most important, she felt, he didn't respect her. And if the man she was falling in love with didn't feel that the way she spent her life was worthwhile, well then, the foundation of that love was made of paper. On the other hand he acted as if he were truly taken with her, had said as much, but it could be just a smooth line. She just didn't know and her head was pounding.

After about fifteen minutes of silence, Jonathan cleared his throat. "It looks like we're in for a hot spell."

Oh no! He wasn't really going to talk about the weather now, she thought frantically. "Yes, it's pretty muggy," she responded in a strained voice.

He turned on the radio, turning the dial till he came to an all-news station. At least there would be no romantic ballads to serenade them on this trip home, she mused in relief. It would be easier to hear about inflation than about someone's "cheating heart." The trouble about this whole affair, she continued in her ruminations, was that it was too unclear. Nothing had been stated. She really had little inkling about how he felt. Did he take her seriously? From the inauspicious start of this relationship, from all his disparaging remarks, it seemed doubtful. But she was a psychologist! she argued with herself. Who should know better than she that it was actions that counted more than words. He had spent grueling days helping her with her apartment. He had cooked for her, sought her out, taken the trouble to find out where she was giving that talk, and had even boned up on the subject of her talk. All of those things spoke far more eloquently than words. Yet she doubted him. The fault must lie within her. She glanced over at him. The steely set of his jaw against the classic perfection of his profile made her heart thump painfully, a condition she was beginning to consider normal. She wanted to reach out and touch his cheek. But she couldn't.

A long time ago, she reminded herself, she had learned not to beg.

The remainder of the ride home was uneventful except for one small event. While they were still in Lancaster County, where most of the Amish lived, they passed a small airport with an enormous sign in front of it.

HOT AIR BALLOON RIDES! it announced. The first ever, open to the public! Only twenty dollars for the most exciting half hour of your life!

As if hesitating Jonathan slowed the car while passing the airport. He sent RoseEllen a fleeting glance. Stepping hard on the gas, he made the car lurch forward.

For the first time in fifteen years RoseEllen bit her nails. He hadn't even asked if she wanted to go for the balloon ride. He had just assumed she would say no.

She couldn't wait to get home. When, after stopping for gas, he went into the rest area, RoseEllen seriously considered running out of the car and hitching a ride with one of the truck drivers whose vehicles dotted the parking lot. Common sense got the better of her. With his return, Jonathan tossed a chocolate bar her way and handed her a Coke.

"Thanks," she murmured as she accepted the soda. She carefully laid the candy bar on top of the brown bag of toiletries. She tried frantically to think of something to say. The tension between them was unnerving. "What if the things you bought at the auction aren't what they're supposed to be? What happens, for example, if the suspenders don't work?"

"If they're not what I bargained for I don't pay," he answered curtly. "Everything put up for auction has certain specs, its written description. There are specifications for size, quantity, type, thickness, tensile strength, purity, and so on, depending on the item. That's the way it is in business. Too bad you can't get specs . . . with other things in life."

"Yes." That was the last conversational gambit she would attempt, she decided.

They lapsed into another silence. This one lasted until Jonathan pulled up at her door.

" 'Bye," she said bleakly.

"Your move," he answered.

"What if I don't play?"

"Not playing is a move." His gaze, as he shifted gears, was hooded.

They looked at each other steadily before he drove off.

RoseEllen felt sick. She felt like clutching her sides and falling to the sidewalk. Instead she walked into her vestibule with all the dignity she could muster and unlocked her mailbox. She withdrew a fistful of letters, none of them junk mail. There was a birth announcement from an old high school chum, a letter from an uncle who had retired to Florida, and two letters from overseas. She sat down on the hallway steps to read them. One was from India. Aruna thanked her for the beautiful dress and in carefully chosen English described her birthday celebration. RoseEllen smiled. The other letter was from Luís, who apprised her (no doubt with the help of a translator who, judging from the illegibility of the missive, had probably flunked English) of the efforts of his small town to build a clinic and told her how much he liked school and how glad he was that she had "adopted" him because now there was always milk and food in the house. Carefully folding the children's letters, RoseEllen slowly climbed the stairs to her apartment. How small her problems seemed in comparison to the problems of these children.

Jonathan loved her, he loved her not. How insignificant. And how good it would be to get back to work on Monday and to the real world. Still, the insistent pressure in her head did not abate.

# CHAPTER EIGHT

RoseEllen Robbins, therapist, wearing a gray linen suit, a burgundy blouse which tied at the neck in a floppy bow, and low-heeled gray lizard pumps, sat facing Pete Mays, her salesman-poet. Despite her urgings, Pete did not feel ready to terminate therapy. There was some controversy in the field about how to deal with such a situation. Some psychologists refused additional therapy to patients who they felt were ready to leave. Others, such as RoseEllen, preferred to ease a patient out gently, letting him know he ought to leave but permitting him to stay on if he felt he couldn't handle the independence. After all, RoseEllen felt, hers was a nurturing profession and you couldn't nurture by refusing aid, even in the name of a higher good. Eventually Pete would realize that he could make it on his own. The fact that his wife had divorced him after thirty years made it all that much more difficult for him to leave the safety of RoseEllen's office. It would be like reliving his divorce. RoseEllen understood that. And despite clinical evidence to the contrary, if Pete felt that he still needed help, he very well might.

"How did you feel when your daughter said you couldn't come over to watch the baseball game?" she probed.

"Kind of bad, I guess," Pete admitted morosely. He wore his sad-dog look. It was an expression he rarely assumed anymore but it had been one of his hallmarks when he first started therapy.

"Why did it make you feel bad?"

"Aw, I don't know."

"How did you feel when she said no?" RoseEllen rephrased the question.

"I guess I felt like a big dope, wanting to butt in on her life. I wanted to break my furniture and bash my head against the wall." He laughed dejectedly.

"Wasn't there anything you wanted to say to her?" RoseEllen tried to redirect his anger to its proper source. Like so many of her patients Pete had a habit of directing his anger inward instead of outward where it belonged.

"Maybe there was, but, well, I forgot it," he finished lamely.

"I'd like to try something with you now, Pete. Let's do a little pretending. I'll be your daughter." She turned around so her back was to him. "Let's have that conversation again."

"I couldn't do that. I'm not much good at playacting. Never was."

"Why don't you let me decide that. That's my job." Sometimes she had to be firm and authoritative. And this was one of those times, RoseEllen reflected. Cupping one fist to her mouth, the other to her ear, she pretended to be talking into a phone. "Hello."

"H-hello," Pete stuttered, clearly feeling foolish.

"Hi, Dad. Could you hold on a minute." She got up, walked over to her bookcase, took out a book and stood idly flipping through it for a full minute. Returning to her chair, she reassumed her earlier position. "What's up, Dad?"

"Nothing much—same old thing. What's new?"

"Lots of things. It would take me forever to explain. You know how I am, Dad, always running. Actually, I've got to go now. I have a racquetball appointment soon."

"Well, um," Pete said hoarsely. "I was wondering, I mean I thought it would be nice if I came over later to watch the game with you. You know, like we did when you were little."

RoseEllen sucked in her cheeks. This was going well. He was entering the fantasy. "That sounds great, Dad, but I really can't today. Maybe some other time, okay? Look, why don't you call one of your buddies or something. I'm sure you can find someone to watch the game with you."

"I wanted to watch it with you," Pete insisted in a voice that had broken.

"Dad! Really! Don't be hokey!" RoseEllen hoped she was doing a good job at imitating a twenty-one-year-old sophisticate.

"I wanted to watch it with you! Dammit!" Pete's voice was rising. "You don't have time for me anymore. Well, little girl, I'm not ready for the glue factory yet! And don't you forget it! When you have a problem, when you have to cry, where are you always going to find a willing ear and a ready shoulder? Here! That's where! Maybe I'm not the world's greatest father—I don't have a lot of money to buy you things—but you'll never find anyone who loves you more. I'm tired of the way you treat me, just the way your mom did. I'm not going to take it anymore." His voice shook. "I'm not going to take it anymore. If you want to see me again you'll have to call me." Pete started to cry. Great sobs shook his massive shoulders.

RoseEllen turned around. Pete Mays was basically a healthy man. Now it was child's play to get him in touch with his feelings, but that had not always been the case. When she had first started with him, he drank a bottle of beer for every sorrow he had and his beer belly stood out a yard in front of him. She handed him a box of tissues.

142

To give him time to compose himself she leaned back in her chair with closed eyes.

"I guess I should have told her all of those things," he said finally.

"There's always next time," RoseEllen soothed. "You said them to yourself. That's most important." She glanced at her watch. "I'm afraid our time is up for today, Pete. See you next week."

"Miss Robbins"—Pete swallowed convulsively—"I think maybe I'll take a few weeks off. See if I can make a go of it on my own. You know what I mean?"

"That's a wonderful idea!" RoseEllen smiled encouragingly. "You'll do just fine!"

Donning the old fedora he always wore, Pete left. RoseEllen smiled a calm, professional smile. When the door closed she jumped up, threw her arms in the air, and stifled a triumphant *Whoopeeeee!* By any definition she had succeeded with Pete Mays. With her help he had walked out of her office a functioning, emotionally sound human being. She paced around her office hugging herself. There was nothing like success!

With a free hour before her next patient, RoseEllen decided on a coffee break. In her reception room she found Wilson busy at his typewriter.

"Why don't you come out with me for a cup of coffee, Wilson?"

"Miss Robbins," he said wearily, "do you have any idea how much mail accumulated during our vacations? When I came back I had twice the amount of work waiting for me! Even after a full week I still don't have it straightened out. It seems like everyone decided to pay their bills—finally."

"That's good news," she kidded him. "It means you get paid! And it means I can afford to buy you that cup of coffee and Danish!"

Rolling his eyes heavenward, Wilson agreed. They went to the Commissary, a chic cafeteria style restaurant renowned for its sinfully delicious desserts. RoseEllen chose a fresh raspberry tart with her coffee. The custard filling was light, the thin blaze of bitter chocolate providing just enough contrast against the sweetness of the custard and the tartness of the berries. The coffee was fresh ground Columbian.

"Ah." She smiled as she interlocked the fingers of her hands in front of her. "There's nothing like good food and a good secretary!"

"I hate to tell you, but this good secretary landed the lead at Grendel's Lair." He named a small South Street theater café. "Rehearsals start next month."

"That's marvelous, Wilson. Congratulations! But," she wailed, "what am I going to do without you?"

"You can get an office temp. I'll be back. I doubt if the show's going to have a twenty-year run! Anyway, it's what goes on behind locked doors that counts and from the looks of Mr. Mays this morning, ya did good!"

Cheered by thoughts of Pete Mays and the show's possible early closing, and immediately guilt-ridden for the latter thought, RoseEllen asked, "How's your chocolate mousse pie? It doesn't look as good as my tart. Wait a minute. Let me get you one of these."

Without waiting for an answer RoseEllen ran to stand at the back of the fast-moving cafeteria line where she picked up another raspberry tart.

"Do you want to fatten me up before I become a starving young actor again?" Wilson asked by way of thanking her. "You know," he said between bites, "there's something different about you. I can't quite put my finger on it."

"What do you mean?"

He shrugged. "If I didn't know better I would say you were in love. You have a kind of glow."

RoseEllen laughed.

Wilson looked up from his mousse and his tart. He narrowed his eyes and said in a most ponderous voice, "Who is he?"

"Nobody. I mean I'm not in love. What does being in love mean anyway?"

Wilson laid his fork down and put his hands on his hips. "You can't work in a psychologist's office without picking up a thing or two. Besides, I have an actor's intuition. Being in love means you're happy and miserable at the same time," he said fliply. "It also means going out for raspberry tarts in the middle of the morning when you normally refuse sugarless gum. Now don't tell me. I'm going to guess." Wilson's eyes lit up. "Me sees a tall, dark stranger who comes barging into your office with a bull story about an emergency. And then me sees an agitated boss with a flushed face and angry eyes. It was a fellow by the name of Jonathan Wood, wasn't it. That wasn't the name he gave but it was the name on the check he paid with. I thought it odd at the time. I'm quite the sleuth, aren't I?" He laughed boastfully.

"It was meaningless, no more than a brief interlude in an otherwise hectic life."

Wilson raised his eyebrows dubiously.

RoseEllen was spared the necessity of elaborating by the arrival at their table of Dr. Riley.

145

"I thought I saw you when I was back there on line," he said as he pulled a chair out for himself. "May I?"

"Of course." RoseEllen nodded. "You know my secretary, Wilson Beck?"

"Indeed. Hello, Wilson."

"Hi."

"You did famously with that paper of yours. I meant to call you and let you know. It's quite a feather in your cap." Turning to Wilson he reiterated, "I bet you didn't know you were working for an expert on paradox therapy."

"I'm not surprised." Wilson smiled.

"Come on, you guys. That's enough flattery. How's the clinic doing?" She addressed Dr. Riley in an attempt to steer the conversation away from herself.

"Fine, fine. What I don't understand," he said, shaking his head, "is why you let that character, Wood, spirit you away so fast. You missed most of the kudos which you well deserved to hear."

"He's not a character," RoseEllen reproved.

Holding one hand next to his head at eye level, Dr. Riley twisted the wrist back and forth in a gesture which indicated to RoseEllen that he thought "character" was the best thing he could say about Jonathan.

"What's that supposed to mean?" she asked hotly.

Dr. Riley took a deep breath. "That man . . ."

Wilson silenced him with a loud clearing of his throat. "It's getting late. You have an appointment in ten minutes," he addressed RoseEllen.

"Oh, right. We'd better get going." As she stood up she turned deliberately to Dr. Riley. "Jonathan Wood is a fine man. He's—he's better than most!"

"You certainly rose to his defense," Wilson remarked

as they headed out of the Commissary. "Riley will be careful next time he makes statements like that. But if that's what you do for a brief, meaningless interlude, what do you do for a meaningful relationship—recite the Gettysburg Address?"

"Wilson," she sighed, "tell me about the play."

"That can wait. Tell me about Jonathan. You look like you need a sympathetic ear."

"I don't know if advising the lovelorn comes with your job description." RoseEllen laughed wanly without breaking her stride.

"Look, I bring you coffee in the morning, don't I? You never heard me complaining and that's not part of my job description either!"

RoseEllen considered his offer for a full minute. She clicked her tongue resolutely. "I'm confused. Sometimes I think I love him but then I think that I don't really know him. I don't understand him. Worst of all I don't know if I trust him completely."

"Did he ever do anything to make you feel that way?"

"Not really, but he's an unknown quantity. We come from different worlds, we have different reference points. Take someone like Pete Mays, my client. I've seen the man once a week for a few months and I can say I know what makes him tick. I know where he's coming from. That's a hell of a lot more than I can say about Jonathan."

"If I were in love with someone," Wilson said gravely, "for sure I wouldn't want to know her every dream and every little demon stalking her subconscious. That's enough to kill and bury any romance." He looked slightly askance. "Are you sure that's what bothering you? Could it be that you're afraid to be in love?"

They were fast approaching the office. RoseEllen slowed her steps.

"I've had that same thought myself. When you've been on your own as long as I have and made a go of it, it's a little scary to think of surrendering your independence."

"Why should you have to surrender anything?" Wilson asked.

"It happens. A relationship means compromise," she answered matter-of-factly.

"Is he worth it to you?" Wilson probed.

"I don't know. Sometimes I'm sure he is, when he's warm and tender and full of surprises. Being with him then is like breaking open a piñata and gathering up the candy. Other times, I think he's unscrupulous and selfish and surely not worth it." She glanced at her watch. "I've got a patient up there whose life needs untangling. Why is it so much easier to solve other people's problems than your own?"

Her next patient was a young woman who suffered from a fear of signing her name in public. It was a phobia which, though seemingly trivial and even comical, made her client's life miserable. Although the problem had its roots deep in the psyche, this patient, talkative and insightful, would be relatively simple to help. The session was a good one. RoseEllen felt that they were making progress.

After the woman left, RoseEllen leaned back in her chair. She picked up the *Welcomat,* the weekly center city newspaper which Wilson had placed on her desk this morning. As usual the paper, with its well-written, lively articles, was enjoyable, until she came to the piece on condo conversion. With trepidation RoseEllen read the article carefully. Though the bias of the writer was obvious to her, RoseEllen found herself agreeing with his point of view and empathizing with the plight of tenants forced out of apartments they had lived in for years. Condo conversion was a get-rich scheme on the part of greedy developers. When Jonathan's name was mentioned in conjunction with Dr. Riley's, she was not surprised. What did surprise her was the sinking feeling in her stomach. This clinched it. There was no point in continuing with Jonathan. It couldn't go anywhere. Morally they were too far apart. Although she had never thought of herself as a bleeding heart type, she strongly believed that you had to be upright, responsible, and compassionate in your dealings, whether on a personal or business level. She respected Jonathan for what he knew but she could not now respect him for what he stood for. Riches were fine but not if they were gotten at the cost of someone else's happiness.

She sighed. If she were a compulsive eater she would gorge herself, she thought. If she were a drinker she would get soused. Too bad she was neither. Maybe she ought to call a friend and go to a movie tonight. A good mystery or tearjerker might take her mind off Jonathan. Picking up her brown leather address book, she thumbed through the pages. There were several people she could call, friends she hadn't seen in a while, but nobody she really wanted to see tonight. She didn't want to answer questions or evade them, and lying was not something she did well. Maybe she ought to go alone. But for some silly reason, she didn't like to go to the movies by herself. A warm body in the next seat was as essential to her as popcorn.

When her last patient of the day left, the driving offender Judge McIntyre had sent her, RoseEllen placed her address book in her desk drawer, stopped at the magazine kiosk in the lobby of her office building, and with her arms full of fashion and beauty magazines, she headed for home.

Although she had no appetite she put a frozen pizza in the oven, changed out of her clothes, kicked off her shoes, and threw on a pair of jeans and a cotton shirt. With uncharacteristic sloppiness RoseEllen left her suit where she had dropped it on her bedroom floor. It had to go to the cleaners anyway, she rationalized. When Dr. Riley had made that nasty remark about Jonathan at the Commissary today, she had set down her coffee cup with such force that it had splashed on her suit. She hadn't even been aware of it at the time.

Flopping in a living-room chair RoseEllen stared at her freshly painted walls. The pleasure she usually got from her apartment was missing this evening. She thumbed through the pile of magazines she had bought, looking with passing interest at the pictures. Neither articles nor short stories piqued her curiosity. The buzzer on her oven went off. With disinterest RoseEllen took out the small pepperoni pizza. With her first bite she wrinkled her nose in distaste. The crust was doughy and the sauce artificial tasting. She drained the glass of orange juice she had poured for herself and threw the pizza in the trash.

When the doorbell rang she ambled over to it. She usually chain locked her door at night and looked through the peephole before answering. But tonight she forgot those lessons and without thinking she flung the door open. She must have suspected, on some subconscious level, she thought later, who it would be.

"Aren't you going to let me in?" Jonathan asked.

RoseEllen stood there looking at him blankly, not sure how she was going to react.

"Hi there," he said more loudly and with imperturbable

cuteness. "Remember me? I'm the guy you made splendid love with last week. Is this how you treat your men?"

"I don't have 'men'!" she hissed, purposely keeping her voice low. "Come on in before you go into details for the benefit of my downstairs neighbor." She stepped aside.

"Nice paint job," he said as he looked around. "You got yourself one terrific painter. Lucky girl."

"I thanked you for that and I really appreciated it, but I hope you don't think one paint job or"—she paused—"anything else gives you carte blanche over my life."

"What the hell are you talking about?" he exploded. "You're so damn analytical you don't see the forest for the trees!"

" 'You don't see the forest for the trees.' Well. Well. At least I don't talk in clichés!" she shot back weakly.

"No, you wouldn't. You're much too educated for that. Everything you say is original and brilliant. Too bad for the rest of us poor schnooks." He turned back toward the door. "I shouldn't have come. Should've listened to my instincts instead." His hand was on the doorknob.

"Jonathan, wait!"

He moved his head to the side so that she could see the quizzical curve of his brow. Putting her hand timidly on his arm, she nonetheless applied considerable pressure. "Don't pay attention to what I said. Can we strike it from the record?"

She could see the play of emotions on Jonathan's face. There was anger, indecision, and hurt. Vulnerability had never been a word she had associated with him. Yet he was vulnerable, at least to her, she thought. "I'm sorry," she whispered. She wondered if he knew how difficult it was for her to say those words. It had always been difficult—maybe because of some lost incident in her childhood.

"Jonathan!" Sliding her hands up his arms she slipped them around his neck, and standing on her toes she pulled his face down toward her.

His lips were cold at first, but she wouldn't release his head. Gradually words assumed less importance as their bodies began their own conversation. He wrapped his arms around her and pulled her even more tightly to him. He gently massaged her lower back and pushed his hands under her belt. Smiling down at her, Jonathan said, "Let's not argue." To signal her agreement RoseEllen laid her head on his chest.

"Would you like something to drink or eat?" RoseEllen said, retreating into the role of pleasant hostess against her will.

"Let's not drink or eat either." Jonathan grasped her hand and walked into the bedroom.

Wordlessly he unbuttoned her shirt, removed her bra, turned her around, and kissed her gently. His jacket against her bare breasts sent strange, arousing sensations through her whole body. He ran his strong hands along her back and pulled her up toward him.

"Finish undressing," he said simply.

She did, as did Jonathan while keeping his eyes fastened on her. They walked toward each other, and put their arms around one another, savoring the feel of skin against skin. Moving almost imperceptibly they kissed lightly, tenderly.

"Jonathan."

He smiled as he knelt, pulling her down onto the plush carpet of the bedroom.

"The bed . . ." she began haltingly.

"Beds are for sleeping." He smiled.

RoseEllen giggled uncharacteristically.

They stretched out against each other, their mouths glued, as Jonathan ran his hand over her breasts, stomach, and hips. RoseEllen clung to him, hungering for every touch of his strong hands.

Jonathan leaned back to see her clearly. "You're beautiful."

RoseEllen smiled and kissed him as he softly caressed her inner thighs. Aching with desire she imagined her white carpet to be a warm, moisture-laden cloud on which they were both floating, high over Philadelphia.

Finally Jonathan entered her slowly and the sensations were exquisite, so exquisite that she almost became alarmed at the pleasure she was experiencing. Jonathan, sensing this, quietly stroked her cheek. "It's okay, darling." She relaxed and wondered momentarily at his sensitivity. Slowly, steadily Jonathan's thrusts erased all concern, all memory, everything except the slowly sharpening focus of sensations. They moved in unison until a sudden, sweet convulsion shook both of them. Holding hands they squeezed tightly as the pleasure washed over them.

Awash in a whirl of emotions, RoseEllen felt her face become wet from tears. Nobody had ever touched her as Jonathan had—deep, deep inside her heart. She was so open to him; she could be so easily wounded. For the first time in her life she felt like a delicate flower, wanting to be treasured and savored. He made her feel beautiful. He colored her in pastels. Brushing away the hairs that had stuck across her cheek, Jonathan wiped at her face with the back of his hand.

"What's the matter?"

"Nothing. It's—it's only that I want it to be perfect with us."

"Woman, if that wasn't perfect, nothing is. We're the right fit." Tenderly he stroked the slight swell of her belly.

"I don't mean only like that," she answered quietly.

"We're working on it." He smiled jauntily.

"I read about you in the paper this morning." RoseEllen bit her lip. This wasn't the time to talk about it but she couldn't help herself. She had to find out from him what he thought about the whole condo scandal.

"Which paper?"

She heard a wariness in his voice. *"Welcomat."*

"Oh, that," he replied with a dismissive wave of his hand. "Forget it."

"Why?" Her voice held a note of hopefulness. "Isn't the article true? It's a good newspaper."

"I thought you were too sophisticated to believe everything you read. Not even *The New York Times* tells the whole truth all of the time."

"I don't want to argue the journalistic merits of newspapers with you," she responded testily, for she felt he was trying to avoid the issue. "I want to know the truth."

"What is truth?" he teased. "I thought you were a psychologist. Now you want to talk philosophy!"

"Jonathan! Don't play games. And I also wish you'd stop joking around about my profession!" She pulled the sheet which she had taken from her bed up to her shoulders.

"You of all people should know there's no such thing as truth," he continued unrelentingly. "It's different for every person. It depends on your perspective."

"So the paper's right!" she gasped. "You are bilking those tenants for every last penny."

Jonathan uttered a small laugh, devoid of all humor. "Honey, why don't you get a couple of glasses of wine and

154

an ashtray? You wouldn't happen to have a copy of *The Total Woman,* would you? If you do, bring that too. There's a couple passages you ought to read, about being supportive."

Hitting the carpet with her fist RoseEllen sat up and shouted, "Stop dancing around it. You're either on the up-and-up or you're a wheeler-dealer who only cares about the bottom line. Which is it?"

"There's no middle ground, I take it?" Jonathan drawled.

There was no doubt about it, RoseEllen fumed. He was baiting her. It was an effective tactic to avoid compromising questions. Never take the defensive. Always attack.

"Maybe there is," she conceded. "All I'm asking is that you explain it to me. And all I'm asking is that you tell me, just one time, that you respect what I do for a living!"

Closing her eyes she begged him silently to tell her that it was all right. When she opened them he was standing, pulling on his pants. With one hand she held the sheet up to her chin, with the other she reached out to rub his back. Horrified, she watched him recoil from her touch.

"Jonathan?" Her voice was high-pitched.

"Be seeing you around. Keep the faith," he answered in a voice heavy with sarcasm.

Draping the sheet around herself toga style, she clambered over the pillows they had strewn here and there on the carpet.

"Don't be angry because I want to talk. It's, pardon the expression, a lack of communication that kills relationships, not the other way around."

Putting two hands on her shoulders he pushed her backwards so that she tripped on one of the pillows. "Cut the jargon, will you? We're not talking about the lack of com-

155

munication here," he mimicked her tone. "We're talking about something a lot more basic—a lack of trust."

"I trust you," she whispered.

"Like you'd trust a cobra," he retorted, "for as long as you're playing the flute."

"That's not true. I've been reading about you and hearing talk about you. I want to hear whatever it is from you, not someone else. Is that so terrible?" she demanded.

"There's more to this interrogation." His smile was thin. "You want to know if I'm a *cad*," he enunciated carefully in a mocking way, "or a *knave* or a *rogue*. Or maybe you want to know if I'm a local gangster. While you're at it why don't you ask if I have toe rot!"

"Don't be ridiculous!" she snapped. "You don't have to make a joke out of everything, you know!" She stepped into her own jeans. Leaving her bra on the floor, she pulled on her T-shirt. With arms folded across her chest she glared at him.

"What if I were to tell you that every innuendo you heard or read about me is true. I care about nothing but the almighty buck. How would that make you feel?"

"I don't know," she answered. "I'd be upset."

"Or what if I were to totally vindicate myself. Show you that I'm a pinch hitter for Albert Schweitzer. How would you feel then?"

"Glad, of course." She was puzzled.

"Lady, nothing, *nothing* is what I'm telling you," he said with an exaggerated swagger to the window. "You take me as I am. I think you should know me well enough by now that these kinds of questions are unnecessary."

"You get more of a guarantee when you buy a pair of shoes," she sniffed. "At least you get to try them on and walk across the room in them. Anyway, I know you're not a philanthropist and I know you're not the Godfather. You fall somewhere in the middle. I want to know which side you're leaning toward. That's not too much to want to know about somebody. I'm not asking to see your IRS records for the past five years. I'm not asking for the story of your life. I just want to know about this condominium deal. I would want to know that much about someone I was going to sublet my apartment to and I don't see what you're so touchy about."

"I see. It goes like this: I plead my case. You sit in judgment. And then I live with your decision. No thanks. I didn't sign up for that."

"You have a great way of twisting things," she shot back. "What it all boils down to is respect. If you had any respect for me and for what I do you'd want to share every part of your life with me—not just selected ones. Well, this has been an eye-opener for me too. I never thought you were the kind of guy who would want his woman barefoot, pregnant, and dumb. Hi-yo, Silver!"

His face mottled from fury, his nostrils flaring, Jonathan picked up a pillow and with all his force threw it against the wall. A small flurry of feathers flew out from the somewhat worn napping.

"I'll bet you wish you were doing that to me instead of a pillow," she taunted.

"Why don't you practice that wonderful insight on your patients instead? Do you sit in judgment of them too? If you don't like their business practices do you kick them out of your office? Or do you reserve that privilege for the bedroom?" he snapped, his angry voice tearing through her.

"I don't sleep with my patients! And stop shouting!" she

yelled in a voice strangulated by tears. She couldn't stand the harshness of his tone, and his lack of understanding.

"Why?" he bellowed. "Can't you take it? Don't you want to finish what you started?"

Pressing her fingertips to her forehead she squeezed her eyes closed as if that would shut out the sound of his voice. "No," she answered calmly. "I don't think we're getting anywhere."

"That's fine by me." He rolled the sleeves of his white shirt up over his bronze forearms and strode from the bedroom.

RoseEllen was right behind him, stalking him. "Let's get one thing straight."

His face stony, his posture rigid, he stood immobile.

"I don't judge my patients," she insisted. "I'm not a judgmental person. But it's different with you." There was a determined tone in her voice.

"Why? Do you think I'm beyond redemption?"

To RoseEllen's ears the bitterness of his voice did not conceal the hurt.

"Of course not! Stop putting words in my mouth. It's different because"—her voice went up an octave—"because . . . I care about you—about us." She looked at her bare feet, noticing for some strange reason that her nail polish was unattractively chipped. "I think I'm in love with you."

Afraid of seeing irony or worse in his eyes she did not look up. For what seemed like a long while he did not respond. When he did, what she refused to see in his eyes she heard in his voice.

"You're in love with me. That's very flattering. But I'm not sure you know what that means. Love, you see, is given completely. If you love somebody you support him;

158

you would walk across the frozen steppes of Russia for him. You would give him the benefit of the doubt. You would believe in him and wouldn't assume the worst about him. You've got a lot to learn—about love—about the world."

"What do you want me to do? Beg your forgiveness? I won't!" She tried, with little success, to sound scathing.

"You're not the type to beg. If you were it wouldn't matter. I think I deserve your trust; I've earned it. I started to tell you once that I was falling in love with you. Something stopped me from pursuing the subject, though."

"What stopped you?" RoseEllen asked with growing trepidation. She didn't know which way this conversation would go and had little control over its outcome. The stakes were high: she was playing with her happiness.

"What stopped me?" He paused to consider. "Oh, maybe the feeling that you weren't ready. I'm older than you, not by much, a few years or so, but enough to recognize what counts. You've been too cloistered in that ivory tower of yours with the swivel chair and the potted palm and that secretary you have, who prances around trying to figure out new ways to tie his neckerchief so he'll impress his directors. I should have known as soon as I saw that you had a male secretary that you had some growing up to do."

"That's not fair. Wilson is an excellent secretary. The fact that he's a man never entered into my decision to hire him," she fibbed.

"Oh? Didn't it give you a small surge of power to be able to have a male secretary?" he asked rhetorically. "But we're getting away from the issue. You still don't trust me.

159

You still don't think I'm quite respectable and you don't think I think you are!"

She opened her mouth to protest.

"Don't say anything." He held up his hand.

Stifling the urge, which dominated her at that moment, to take that hand and press it to her lips, to tell him that she didn't care what he did or how he did it, took all her willpower.

"You're kind of self-righteous," he continued, "but if we take you apart and examine some of your motives I'm not so sure you'd come out spanking clean. Perfect people are hard to live with."

"I never said I was perfect. And we never talked about living together. You're exaggerating this whole thing and you know it. Maybe you have other reasons. Maybe you're not so sure about us either," she challenged, defiance in her tone.

"Maybe," he agreed cuttingly. His mouth looked cruel, the black centers of his eyes shone like obsidian. "For a while there I thought I was sure. But you're right. I'm not sure anymore, despite your pretty avowal of love—maybe everlasting, maybe not," he added facetiously. He looked suddenly tired. "I'm going home now, RoseEllen."

Though she wasn't looking at herself in a mirror, RoseEllen knew she was pale. There was nothing she could do to stop him. At that moment she didn't want him to stay. All she wanted was to curl up in bed and pull the covers up over her head—after she put on some sheets. To say she was hurt by his words, she thought as she watched the door slam behind him, was an understatement. She was stricken.

# CHAPTER NINE

Never having paced before in her life, RoseEllen found herself walking up and down, back and forth, across her living room. Having wandered into the bedroom, she hadn't the heart to remain there for more than a minute. A faint, musky, male scent lingered in the air. She closed the door.

Plopping heavily on her living room sofa she drew her knees up to her chin. It was true what they said about stress: it hurt. Every muscle in her body ached, especially her neck and back muscles. The headache which had started over the bridge of her nose was making her entire skull throb and her vision blurry. She blinked rapidly and focused her eyes on the floor. What a great job he had done for her on the floors. A great floor job, great paint job, great snow job! She had to get out of here!

Grabbing the muted pink, zippered summer jacket she liked to wear with jeans, she transferred her keys, a couple of dollars, and a small pack of Kleenex from her bag to her back pocket. Somehow she knew she was going to take a long walk with shoulders hunched and hands in pockets. She wouldn't want to be bothered with the straps of a bag slipping off her shoulder. It was weird, she thought, how in the midst of a crisis, a trauma, her mind could function so rationally about such piddling things.

The cool night air slapped against her cheeks. She took a deep breath which, for all her stifled tears, she felt sharply in her chest. The day's heavy traffic fumes having dissipated, the air was fresh and sweet. She headed west along

Pine Street with its antique shops shuttered behind steel grills, its darkened ice cream shops which sold cones with flavors like Grand Marnier chip for a dollar and fifty cents, extra if you wanted sprinkles, and its newly opened restaurants and cafés, one on almost every block it seemed. Philadelphia, in the last few years, had been undergoing a restaurant renaissance so that if you wanted a plain bowl of spaghetti and sauce in a decent-looking place you would be hard pressed to find pasta that wasn't green and made of artichokes and floating around in capers and cream sauce. The infamous remarks that W. C. Fields had made about Philadelphia came to her mind: that he would rather be dead in Los Angeles than alive in Philadelphia, and that he went to Philadelphia the other night—and it was closed. W. C. Fields would be singing a different tune if he were alive today, she thought.

Touching her fingers to her face she was surprised to find it wet with tears. It was a fine state of affairs to be crying and not even know it, she thought as she exhaled heavily. Why did it have to end like this? Maybe Jonathan had been on target about her—maybe it was she who was in need of a rehaul. Maybe she was a prissy, narrow-minded fuddy-duddy. Maybe, maybe, maybe. On the other hand he was a secretive and private person. How could he expect her to share her life with him if he didn't share his with her?

Sometimes she got the feeling that what was important to him was a good time, that he wanted her when he wanted her. If all she had meant to him was fun and laughs, that's all he would mean to her. For her to love someone it would have to be a total commitment, a total sharing. Of course, she could only have that with someone who was like her in manner, thought, and integrity. So,

162

she scolded herself, what was she bawling about? For she had started crying out loud now, not caring who heard her or what they thought. From one pocket she took fresh Kleenex, into the other she stuffed wet, crumpled ones. She should never have gone to Dr. Riley's party in the first place. Then she wouldn't have met Jonathan and her life would have been so much simpler. And so much more boring, a voice in the back of her mind (her id, she thought wryly) spoke up.

Having walked halfway across town, RoseEllen came to Rittenhouse Square, a lovely, turn-of-the-century type square, with benches, pigeons, and women in mink or derelicts in rags equally at home there. Surrounded by some of the city's most elegant hotels and apartment buildings, it was at the same time continental and chic, yet distinctly Philadelphian. There was a take-out place across the street where you could buy curried chicken salad for an outdoors lunch on a Rittenhouse bench and there was a stand on the corner where you could buy hot pretzels slathered with mustard.

Starting at one end, RoseEllen slowly toured the empty square. She wasn't afraid of the solitude and the night for hundreds of windows, like so many watchful eyes, looked down on her. As she walked, pigeons fluttered and flew before her, affronted that a human dared to disturb their quietude.

"Miss Robbins!" From the shadows a portly figure rose from a bench. "What are you doing here?"

Before she saw him she recognized the nasal twang. "Pete Mays! I could ask the same of you!"

"I like the square at night," he said. "It's peaceful and beautiful in a way it can't be when the sun is shining."

"You're right, and poetic as ever. Well! How are you

doing, Pete?" she asked in her best professional voice, having managed to stem her flood of tears. Taking a tissue from her pocket, she dabbed at her left eye, which always was the teariest one, pulling the lid down and pretending that a fleck of dust had flown in.

"Why, Miss Robbins," Pete Mays exclaimed in a voice grown gentle, "you're crying!" Taking a big white handkerchief from his pocket he handed it to her awkwardly. "Why don't you sit down with me and talk about it? It will do you good to get it out of your system."

The solicitousness of his gesture and his voice made RoseEllen's tears redouble. He was so kind, this Pete Mays, she thought, and he sure wasn't going to charge her fifty dollars for listening to her tale of woe.

"It's a man, isn't it?" he asked. When she didn't respond he continued, "If he's doing this to you he's not worth it. Any man who could hurt you . . ."

"It's not like that," RoseEllen interrupted. "It was all my fault." She stopped in mid-thought. What had she said?

"Ah hah!" Pete nodded knowingly. "Then what are you doing here? You should be telling him that instead of me."

"It's not so simple," RoseEllen mumbled. "Pete"—she stood up—"it's kind of you to want to listen but I really shouldn't be talking to you like this."

He stood up next to her. "Let's walk around the square. I can see maybe you're embarrassed and all, what with you being a psychologist. But don't think about it. Everyone needs a friendly ear now and then." He shook his head. "You're still young. When you're as old as I am you'll know that it doesn't matter who you are. We're all made the same."

Her pulse quickened. This was the second time in one

night she had been told she was young. At the age of twenty-eight she wasn't accustomed to thinking of herself in those terms. But maybe there was a brittle, callow edge to her.

"Pete." She smiled. "I usually don't tell my patients this, or my ex-patients, but you're a genuinely nice guy."

"But nice guys finish last," he said resignedly. "It's true. I've always been a nice guy, a real nice minor character in a lot of people's lives. Ah well, RoseEllen. I can call you RoseEllen, can't I?"

"Sure."

"RoseEllen, if you love this guy don't let anything stand in your way. It's not easy to come by love and nothing else counts for near as much. When you're alone at night all the success in the world won't warm you, the way all the brandy in the world can't warm me." He looked up at the black sky. "It's love that counts."

She looked at Pete Mays intently. She saw the bulbous nose, the jiggly jowls, and thought that there stood a beautiful person. She heard the clichés he uttered and thought that from him they sounded earnest and rang true. She put a hand on his arm.

"If you ever need to talk give me a call—unofficially."

"I just might do that sometime. You're good at what you do and you helped me face a lot. I don't think I'll ever need 'official' help again, but well, an objective, smart lady to listen on occasion, who would say no to that? I hope you straighten out your own life. Maybe it seems to you that you've got all the time in the world now but you'd be surprised at how fast it flies. This fellow of yours—if he can make your eyes red and pained like that he must be pretty special."

"He is pretty special," she gulped.

"Then go to him."

She inclined her head and chewed on her bottom lip. "Maybe you're right. I think I'll call him first."

"There's a phone booth across the street." Pete pointed helpfully. "Do you need a dime?"

Checking her pockets RoseEllen pulled out her two dollar bills. "Do you have change?"

Pete laughed as he handed her a dime and a nickel in case she ran overtime.

"You can buy me a cup of coffee sometime. I'll wait here while you call," he offered kindly.

As RoseEllen reached out to push on the streaked, murky glass of the phone booth her ears were assailed by the shriek of rusty hinges and her nose by the musty odor of stale air. Her fingers were clammy as she dialed Jonathan's number. The phone rang once, twice, six times. She hung up.

"Well, what happened?" Pete asked as she crossed back to the square.

"Nothing. He wasn't home." She hung her head dejectedly until she realized what she was doing. She smiled brightly at Pete.

"I'm going to head on home now. Thanks." Impulsively she bent over to kiss the vein-crossed cheek.

"How about that cup of coffee?" Pete asked concernedly. "I'm buying."

"I'll take a rain check on that. It's getting late and . . . I should be getting home to sleep."

"Let me walk you back. You aren't safe, alone at night on the streets."

"I'll be fine. Don't worry. Believe me, I'm street-wise. I always walk fast and where it's well lit. Anyway," she confided, "I took a karate course once and I'm not too bad at it."

Pete chuckled. "You're quite a lady."

The walk back to her apartment was negotiated quickly. The anxiety she felt was translated into a surge of energy and if this were a walking race she might have won, she thought at one point. The lights were on in her apartment as she had left them. The bed was still in the same disarray, almost stripped. The floor was a mess of sheets and pillows. The only thing which stood out for its neatness was the paint job on her walls which, she mused, had unfortunately not chipped off in great chunks.

As soon as she hung up her jacket and drank a glass of cold water, she kneeled on the floor near her telephone and dialed Jonathan's number. Again there was no answer. Dialing information she got his business number. His answering service said that his offices were closed until nine o'clock the next morning. She had expected that. Maybe she ought to practice a karate chop on herself, she thought glumly. What a fool she had been. Pete Mays had been right. Love is what counts. And she did love Jonathan. She did. Without him the life which had once seemed so full to her now loomed empty. So what if she wouldn't handle business the way he did? How could she say what she would do anyway? It was a world far removed from hers and a world which she didn't understand. It was a world which he, however, was able to command. Knowing him she didn't believe, despite what Dr. Riley and the newspaper had insinuated, that he would purposely manipulate his affairs to hurt other people. Why hadn't she realized that before she had spoken? Why hadn't she conveyed that trust to him? Because, she answered herself, she hadn't thought it out. As usual she had been unfairly opinionated with little basis for being so. Perhaps that was an occupational hazard.

If only it wasn't too late! If only he were home! She would tell him, explain to him that she had been wrong. Nothing mattered, she would say, except him and her. As for his psychology jokes, she could take them! And she wouldn't care if he never went to an opera or a ballet. She wouldn't care if he wanted to play country-western all night long—as long as she had her earplugs. Whatever it was, they could work it out. And she knew, she really did believe, that business couldn't work on compassion alone. She trusted him. She had to make him believe that.

She tried his house again and again. At two o'clock in the morning he had still not returned, or else he wasn't answering. Finally, with the help of a warm glass of milk and two aspirins, she fell into a fitful sleep, curled up on the sofa near the phone.

The sun, streaming in through her undrawn vertical blinds, woke her up at eight thirty the next morning. Her first appointment was in half an hour and she knew she'd never make it in time. Groping groggily in the kitchen cabinets she made herself a quick cup of instant coffee. When she first awakened she had experienced a vague feeling of dread. It took the first sip of coffee to bring the events of the previous day into focus. Draining her cup she headed for the phone. He was still not home. The misery of the night before was replaced by a new worry. Where had he spent the night? And with whom? *There!* she scolded herself. She was doing it again, thinking mean, mistrustful thoughts. This had to stop!

Dressing quickly, RoseEllen chose a navy-and-white seersucker suit with a white tailored blouse. The blouse came with a navy velvet ribbon which she ran under the collar and tied in a bow over her top button. Very businesslike, she thought, as she surveyed herself in the mirror. She frowned and with a quick movement she pulled off the ribbon and unbuttoned her top two buttons. She threw her jacket on the bed, undid her cuffs, and folded them up once. Though for the first time in her career she would undoubtedly wind up a few minutes late, she decided she would follow her daily routine of walking to work and enjoy the summer morning.

She had an easy day at the office in spite of arriving late for her first appointment. Her two other morning clients were sent by Judge McIntyre as part of his good driving habits program. As much as RoseEllen could turn off her personal life when in the office she was glad that today's sessions would require little concentration. The deconditioning which she had to provide consisted of little more than preprogrammed materials. During the entire two hours of the sessions her fingers itched to call Jonathan. As soon as the last client left she began calling again. When he didn't answer she called his business number. It made a lot more sense calling at eleven o'clock in the morning than in the wee hours. To her query his secretary answered that Mr. Wood wasn't in this morning and wouldn't be back until the afternoon. Could she take a message?

"No, thank you. Is there any way I can reach him? Can you tell me where he is?" RoseEllen asked politely, trying to keep the desperation out of her voice.

"I'm sorry," his secretary answered firmly.

"It's important," RoseEllen insisted.

The secretary hesitated. "Is this of a personal nature?"

"Yes."

"I really shouldn't. It's against policy."

"Please," RoseEllen now pleaded, not caring if she did sound desperate.

"Well, all right," she relented. "I'll tell you but I don't want to get in trouble for this."

"Absolutely not," RoseEllen assured her gratefully. "Where is he?"

"He's at the South Street Boys Club. He'll be there till twelve."

"The South Street Boys Club? Thanks."

As she left her office she checked with Wilson. There was definitely nothing on the agenda for the rest of the day except that she had to return an urgent phone call from Dr. Riley.

"Would you get him on the phone for me, Wilson?"

Her secretary nodded, looked up the number in the revolving file, dialed, and handed the receiver to RoseEllen.

"RoseEllen here, Dr. Riley," she spoke crisply. "What can I do for you?" She listened intently. "Chair the paradox theory seminars at the national family therapy conference!" she repeated in awestricken tones. "That's quite an honor. Why me?"

"That's awfully nice to hear," she laughed in response to what Dr. Riley had said. "When is it?"

"Oh no," she groaned. "Next month in Los Angeles. That would be rough for me. Yes, I know it's a phenomenal opportunity and I know it will get me wide renown, but let me think about it, will you? I'll get back to you."

She hung up the phone, looked at Wilson, and decided she couldn't do it. If anything were going to come of this thing with Jonathan—she knew that after what had occurred a happily-ever-after ending was iffy at best—it would happen soon, this summer. She couldn't risk it. Pete Mays was right. Success didn't keep you warm at night.

"Wilson, call Dr. Riley back for me, will you? Tell him I'm sorry but I can't do it. Maybe next year. Never mind, I'll call and tell him no."

Wilson scowled. "Are you feeling all right? I can't believe you'd pass this up when everybody else is fighting over chairmanships of the seminars. You are really changing! Are you going through a mid-life crisis about twenty years too early?"

"Don't be fresh!" she laughed. "All that's happening is that I'm learning that being perfect isn't necessarily perfect. I'm leaving now. Why don't you take the rest of the day off? Call the service and tell them to take calls."

"Yes, *ma'am*," he said gleefully, "and here's to imperfection!" He lifted an imaginary wineglass in a toast.

"You didn't take your briefcase," Wilson remarked as they walked together out of the building.

"No." She smiled. "I didn't." Stepping out into the street she hailed a passing taxi. "South Street Boys Club," she told the cabbie.

What in the world was he doing there? she thought as the taxi sped off. If he wanted to work out, the snazzy Philadelphia Athletic Club would be much more appropriate for one who drove a Porsche, she thought with an ironic chuckle. The Boys Club was more disreputable-looking than even she had imagined. It was in a delapidated building in a run-down neighborhood of half burned-out row houses. Until she had come to Philadelphia, RoseEllen had never seen a row house—those curious two- and three-story homes that were connected to one another for the length of an entire city block.

Rifling in her bag for her wallet, she read the taxi's

meter. It said $5.35. She hastily figured the tip by her rule of thumb—15¢ on the dollar. Suddenly it made no difference. "Keep the change," she told the driver as she handed him a ten-dollar bill.

Stepping gingerly from the cab to the curb, she made sure to miss stepping in the pile of trash in the gutter as she pressed her bag more firmly to her side. Maybe she wasn't crossing the frozen steppes of Russia for him, she thought wryly as she recalled his words, but this was close enough.

The building smelled of mildew and Lysol spray. It reverberated with the sounds of basketballs bouncing on wooden floors, sneakered feet jumping, and the referee's whistle.

"Hey, Salazar! That's foul. . . ." Jonathan's voice echoed through the ground floor of the building.

As she turned the first corner RoseEllen came to the doorway of a cavernous gymnasium. It was filled with young boys, not more than nine or ten years of age. Jonathan, in a regulation gray sweat suit, was demonstrating a hook shot. With no other adults present he was clearly in charge. The boys encircled him, respectfully watching him angle and leap for the basket.

"You try that now, Chuck." He threw the ball at a slight, tow-haired boy.

Stepping behind the door RoseEllen peeked out stealthily. Instinct told her to remain hidden.

"Terrific," he encouraged the boy. "Can you do that again?"

With a face that mirrored his concentration, the boy took the ball, leaped, and made another basket.

"Way to go!" Jonathan cheered.

172

"Can I try that, Coach?" a small boy, who RoseEllen had noticed hanging back, piped up.

"Sure thing!" Jonathan's voice was jocular.

RoseEllen couldn't help but smile to herself. The boys looked so serious and so respectful, as if Jonathan were the greatest thing to ever have walked into their lives. If anybody had said she was spying she knew she would be hard put to defend herself. She ought to leave but she didn't want to. Never having seen Jonathan in this role as benefactor, philanthropist, good guy, it was a revelation to her and it filled her with an emotion she couldn't name. At the same time joy and pride, guilt and shame, battled in her heart. How wrong she had been. How quick she had been to believe in Jonathan's selfishness. Her eyes moist, RoseEllen thought that true altruism was Jonathan's brand—and her own—of do your good deed and don't talk about it. She had wanted him to tell her everything. Strangely, if he had done that he would have, in some small way, diminished his good acts. To be coach to a group of underprivileged children was undeniably praiseworthy, but to be coach and not to tell anyone, not to reap the rewards of society's approval—that was noble.

And at the end of it all—how dashing and desirable he looked in his torn, baggy sweat shirt!

She slunk out. She had seen enough.

## CHAPTER TEN

RoseEllen looked at her watch and then up at the tall gray office building in center city which housed Jonathan's business. One o'clock. He would surely be back at the office now. After having spent a good part of the morning coaching basketball, lunch would certainly be no more than a hastily grabbed sandwich. Never having been to his office, RoseEllen wasn't sure what to expect, though she imagined an open room with crates and cartons and white-shirted clerks wearing black visors and vests. When she thought about it she wasn't sure if clerks anywhere except in the movies dressed like that.

The lobby directory said the Wood Enterprises (rather a pretentious name, she mused) was on the second floor. It didn't give a number. She was the only passenger in the elevator, a good thing considering the mirrored tiles which covered all four walls and gave off the dizzying effect of reflecting her image countless times over, one likeness behind the other. Were the elevator to be crowded and had it gotten stuck, group hysteria would have been difficult to stave off. The sensation was eerie. The designer of this elevator, she decided, had to have been high on drugs or schizophrenic!

When the elevator door opened she found herself in the center of a carpeted salon with a heavy crystal chandelier and Chippendale chairs. A secretary, wearing what RoseEllen would swear was a genuine Chanel suit, sat behind a mahogany desk. Smiling efficiently at RoseEllen she asked if she could be of help.

"Can you tell me where to find Mr. Wood's office?"

"Is he expecting you?" the secretary asked, referring to her appointment book.

"No, but if you can point the way I'm sure he'll see me."

"I'm sorry," she said briskly. "Mr. Wood can't be disturbed. If you'd like to make an appointment . . ."

"Will you tell him I'm here? There won't be a problem."

Raising her eyebrows, the secretary shrugged. "Who shall I say is here?"

"RoseEllen. Tell him RoseEllen wants to see him."

The tone in the secretary's voice was deferential as she spoke to Jonathan through her receiverless phone.

"You can go right in. Follow me." She looked at RoseEllen appraisingly. "Did you call earlier this morning?"

"Yes." RoseEllen smiled.

She followed the woman down a thickly carpeted corridor to a heavy wooden door. The secretary rapped sharply and opened the door wide. She stood aside so RoseEllen could enter.

Feeling a bit like Orphan Annie in the ultra-plush surroundings, she gasped. There was Jonathan standing behind a mammoth glass-and-marble desk. He wore a camel sport jacket, brown slacks, and a cream-colored tie. He bore little resemblance to the man she had just seen cavorting around a dilapidated gym.

"Hello." His voice had the same resonance which had struck her the first time he had ever spoken to her.

"Hello." She walked nearer to where he stood. "I came to say I'm sorry."

"What about?"

"The condo thing. I shouldn't have assumed the worst about you."

"Forget it. No harm done," he said coolly.

"You're still angry. Well, I don't know what to say." She looked around. "This is quite impressive, this office of yours."

"Sorry," he said curtly.

"I didn't mean anything by it. Impressive is a neutral word. I like your office. Now you're going to start reading things into everything I say." She felt her knees trembling. "If anyone has something to complain about it's me. You weren't straight with me from the beginning—passing yourself off as some sort of ragpicker! I hope you found it all very amusing! And by the way, where did you spend last night?"

"It's none of your business," he shot back. "You have no right to ask that question. But for the record, I was at my mother's house. Did you come here to fight? There's no reason for it. You win," he conceded wearily.

With fists clenched at her side, RoseEllen briefly closed her eyes. "I don't want to fight either," she stammered.

He searched her face intently. "Why did you come?"

"I told you"—her voice was like a sob—"to apologize. I don't believe you would do anything unethical. I wanted to tell you that."

"Thanks for the vote of confidence," he returned evenly, though annoyance flashed across his carefully composed features.

"Why don't we wipe the slate clean?" she suggested tentatively. "The mistake I made was not asking the questions I had about you from the beginning. Instead, I answered them for you. Let's talk about it somewhere, maybe over drinks."

"I'm busy, RoseEllen. Some other time."

Incredulous, she stared at him. He didn't believe her.

Could he know how hard it had been for her to apologize to him in the first place? And now he let her humiliate herself in front of him! She had to get out of there!

"If that's the way you want it," she answered coldly, turning with deliberate nonchalance to leave. She felt his eyes following her out.

After leaving Jonathan's office, RoseEllen walked aimlessly around the city. She thought and thought and came to one conclusion. He was justified in his anger and he still cared about her. It had been hurt that she had read in his eyes, legitimate hurt. She was the one who had rebuffed him. And she had done it more than once. She had found a thousand obstacles to put in his way. She had been, to put it kindly, stiff-necked. She knew what she had to do. To let him walk out of her life now would be crazy. There had never been another man for her like Jonathan Wood. There never would be again. She had to try and fix it. True, it might not work. She might be embarrassed. She might feel like a fool. She might wind up rejected. But there came a time when you had to take risks. This was it for her. For too long she had played it safe.

She took a bus to the garage where she parked her Volvo. The only way to have a car in the city, she felt, was to maintain a space near home where a flat monthly rate was paid. Because of the parking problem RoseEllen rarely used her car in town, preferring public transportation. When she did use it, about once a week, she was generally going out of town. Though she loved the city, she regularly felt the need to drive to wide open spaces, where the greenery was not confined to carefully selected spots every twenty yards or so.

As she slipped behind the wheel, she checked the gas gauge. Only half full. She drove to the gas pump at the front of the garage, which was one of the amenities provided for its high-paying renters. Her oil checked, her tank filled, she drove off. Her watch said two. Time was running out and she had a lot to get done.

"Mr. Wood will be leaving at five o'clock. Sorry," the secretary responded in her clipped tones.

*So much the better,* RoseEllen thought as she hung up. It was, she had to admit, adolescent to call his secretary under the guise of wanting an appointment to see her boss at five thirty, just so she could get an idea of what time he left. On second thought, that type of adolescent behavior was exactly the thing that had gotten him in to see her that seemingly long-ago day in her own office.

Hurrying back to her car, she wiped her brow. The last couple of hours had been nothing if not hectic. Praying that this was where he kept his car, she nosed her vehicle to the side of the garage which belonged to Jonathan's building. It was a quarter to five and a steady stream of cars began to exit to make their way home. Mostly they were Fords, Chevrolets, small economy models, but not a single white, slung-back Porsche was in sight. She wiped the small beads of perspiration from the tip of her nose.

Five o'clock came and went and the exhaust from all the tail pipes which blew into her face was beginning to make her eyes smart. She switched her car radio on, played it for ten minutes, and fearing that her battery would weaken, shut it off. Finally, when she thought that maybe he had shinnied down a rope hanging from the side of his building and hopped a passing hansom, he was in front of her in his sparkling automobile. Hurriedly turning the ignition key she slid down in her seat and hoped that he was not a rear-view mirror watcher. She allowed a car to get in between them and decided that if she had to, she would jump red lights to keep from losing him. It turned out that the worst she had to do was to go through two yellow lights. Following was easier than she had imagined and there was no indication that he had spotted her. It was easy, that is, while they remained in the city with its bumper-to-bumper traffic. As Jonathan headed toward the industrial edge of the city where the streets were emptier she knew she would be seen. Now was the moment to act.

Leaning on her horn she zoomed up behind him, her fender almost touching his. Jonathan looked up sharply in his mirror and waved as he recognized her. Swerving sharply from behind she pulled up next to him.

"Pull over," she shouted.

"I can't. I'm late," he answered.

RoseEllen moved her steering wheel a fraction so that the nose of her car was a hairbreadth from his trunk.

"Move over or you'll get your paint scraped," she shouted with a smile.

With an exasperated scowl he complied.

"Now what?" he queried in a ho-hum voice.

"Park, put your keys in your pocket, and come on in." She pushed open the passenger door.

"RoseEllen, I don't have time for this now."

"Listen, mister," she said out of the corner of her mouth in her best imitation of an old-time gun moll, "it's your paint job, your life, or your company. What'll it be?"

With a bemused half-smile, Jonathan got in. Stepping on the gas she roared off.

"What are you up to? I have a business appointment and if you don't stop this nonsense you're going to make me late."

"Call and cancel," she advised as she headed onto the Schuylkill Expressway.

"I don't want to cancel," came his annoyed response. "Just what are you up to?"

She didn't answer right away. Pressing the gas pedal almost to the floor the Volvo leaped forward, weaving in and out of lanes, passing trucks, cars, and motorcycles.

"We have to talk," she said tersely.

"What about?"

"The Phillies," she giggled. "Do you think they'll win the pennant this year?"

"Sure. Carlton's pitching well." He smirked. "Now that we've got that settled how about releasing me? Kidnapping is a federal offense."

In response she pushed even harder on the accelerator, jumping from fifteen to twenty miles over the speed limit.

"Your Judge McIntyre isn't going to be too thrilled when he gets you in his courtroom for reckless driving. He's liable to enroll you in your own driving program. And when I get the opportunity I'm liable to put you over my knee."

"That's a chance I'll have to take," she laughed. "It seems to me that I threatened you with Judge McIntyre once." Glancing at the gas gauge she was relieved to see that it was only down halfway.

"Is this the same RoseEllen Robbins I know?" he asked with a narrowing of eyes, "the RoseEllen Robbins who used automatic *and* hand signals when making a turn? The RoseEllen Robbins who never failed to say please, thank you, and bless you? The same one who pursed her lips at anything off-color even when she thought it was funny? Is this the same RoseEllen Robbins who is driving like a maniac and won't say where? Will you slow down, at least?" he pleaded.

"Don't worry. I'm a good driver."

"I am worried," he snapped. "About your sanity. This has all been very funny, but you can carry a joke too far."

"Who's joking? Why don't you sit back and enjoy the ride?"

"RoseEllen!" he exploded. "Cut it out. Turn off at the next exit and take me back to my car. Of all the hare-brained schemes! What are you trying to prove, anyway?"

"That I trust you," she stated calmly.

"That you trust me! Great! But I don't know if I trust you . . . especially not at seventy-five miles an hour." He paused and looked at her suspiciously. "Did you have something to drink?"

"No." She laughed.

A light seemed to dawn in his eyes. "Did you read the business section of the *Inquirer* today?"

"No, why?" She glanced at him inquiringly.

"You didn't read the article about me?"

"Uh uh." She shook her head adamantly. "What did it say?"

"It vindicated me of any charges in the condo affair. The whole thing, the paper said, was the work of a couple of rabble-rousers who feed on controversy. I had my secretary send my ol' buddy, Riley, a copy. That man should stay with psychology. He's not cut out for business. I have an extra copy in my pocket. You can read it for yourself later."

"Oh, Jonathan!" She turned to him, beaming. "I'm so glad. . . ."

"Keep your eyes on the road!" he shouted.

"Don't have an apoplectic fit. I'm doing fine. That's

181

really wonderful news," she enthused. "Now your reputation is cleared."

"It was always clear," Jonathan observed pointedly.

"Well, of course. I mean . . ."

"Until the next scandal. Is that what you mean?"

"No, no," RoseEllen mumbled.

"There will always be people who want to shed the worst possible light on things and others who will believe anything they read," he added.

Each of his words struck her like a gunshot. Afraid she would cry, RoseEllen chose to say nothing. Her hands tightened their grip on the steering wheel. Maybe she was wrong to be doing this. It wasn't a well-thought-out plan. It was, she admitted to herself, a desperate act by a desperate woman. She had to go through with it. Hadn't he just made it clear that she had nothing to lose except her pride? Pride was a small price to pay in this gamble.

Where the expressway ended she made her way to the Pennsylvania Turnpike, following the route which Jonathan had previously negotiated. After only two exits she headed off the turnpike and down the familiar country roads.

"Did you bring me all the way out here for some authentic Pennsylvania Dutch funnel cake?" Jonathan asked laconically.

"No," she answered shortly, still not trusting herself to speak. She looked at her watch. Six fifteen. She had made good time. Grateful for her unerring sense of direction, she made a right turn, two lefts, went five hundred yards, and pulled over to the side of the road.

"This looks strangely familiar," Jonathan remarked in a puzzled tone, though a glimmer of understanding shone in his eyes as he followed her out of the car.

"Seen one wheatfield and you've seen them all," she bantered nervously as she plunged through the high beige stalks. "Won't you follow me?"

"How could I resist?"

Walking through the wide field, RoseEllen brushed at the wheat that tickled. Almost at the spot where they had lain before and fought before RoseEllen had, hours earlier, spread a chenille blanket on the soft earth. She had planted a bottle of champagne there in a Styrofoam ice bucket, along with a straw basket filled with wrapped delicacies which she had purchased at sinful expense from a take-out gourmet-eria.

Kicking off her mud-caked shoes, she moved to the center of the blanket and, with her eyes on his face, she unbuttoned the third button of her blouse.

"And they say people don't change," he muttered as he stared.

The fourth button—the fifth—she slipped the blouse down over her shoulders and threw it to the side.

Jonathan stepped forward, put his arms around RoseEllen, and pulled her to the blanket.

"I suppose my appointment can wait." He grinned.

RoseEllen tugged at his belt buckle. Obliging her, he undid the buckle, removed his pants, and pulled her skirt up over her hips. The tingle of his legs against hers made her head swoon with sensory delight. She wanted this man, this so-called junkman, more than she had wanted anything or anyone before.

They struggled to remove the rest of their clothes, finally separating for a second to get out of them, then throwing them onto the wheat stalks where they hung looking like scarecrows.

Jonathan laughed. "Looks like they're watching us."

"Let them watch."

RoseEllen dropped to her knees and pulled Jonathan down to his. Facing each other, their bodies grazing each other in the warm August heat, they looked deeply into each other's eyes.

"I love you, RoseEllen."

"I love you, Jonathan."

"Let's drink to that." Jonathan reached for the bottle of champagne and poured out two glasses. "Dom Pérignon! What happened to Great Western?"

"You've taught me a few things."

"I see, I see." He raised the glass. "To us and our long marriage."

"To us and," RoseEllen faltered as tears welled in her eyes, "our long marriage."

Laying aside their emptied glasses, they savored once again the feel of skin, blanket, and the heavy, redolent air.

"Jonathan, I thought you were so annoyed with me, with my . . ." RoseEllen stammered.

"Shh. Where is it written that a man can't sometimes be a little annoyed at the woman he loves, the woman he's going to marry?"

He gently cupped her breast and whispered, "I want to make love to you, RoseEllen Robbins Wood."

"And I want you to, my junkman, my love."

They stretched out next to each other as Jonathan covered her face, neck, and ears with kisses.

Jonathan's proposal had moved her profoundly and now she was being further overwhelmed by his physical presence. The masculine smell of his after-shave, mingled with the champagne on his breath and the fertile aroma of the rich earth, transported RoseEllen to a dizzy, yet delicious state of passion.

His hands roamed her pliant, eager body, working their way with steady, almost maddening deliberation to her thighs. Moaning softly, RoseEllen wrapped her arms and legs about him as Jonathan entered at a tantalizing slow rate.

"Oh, Jonathan," was all that she could say, all she would ever need to say.

# Candlelight Ecstasy Romances

# Quinn

## Sally Mandel

Will Ingram gave Quinn Mallory his heart and soul, but he couldn't sell her his dream of a quiet life in Idaho. She wanted the excitement and adventure of the big city. When Quinn's dream of a television career begins to come true, she is torn between the life she craves and the man she loves. "A cross between *Love Story* and *The Way We Were*."
— *Library Journal*  **$3.50**

# THE TAMING

## Aleen Malcolm

Cameron—daring, impetuous girl/woman who has never known a life beyond the windswept wilds of the Scottish countryside.

Alex Sinclair—high-born and quick-tempered, finds more than passion in the heart of his headstrong ward Cameron.

Torn between her passion for freedom and her long-denied love for Alex, Cameron is thrust into the dazzling social whirl of 18th century Edinburgh and comes to know the fulfillment of deep and dauntless love. **$3.50**